the LANGUAGE of BIRDS

The Language of Birds

Tall Tales from the Old North

by

IAN CUMPSTEY

Northern Displayers, Skadi Press

CUMBRIA, ENGLAND

2025

The Language of Birds

Published in 2025 by Northern Displayers, Skadi Press, England
www.northerndisplayers.co.uk

ISBN 978-0-9576120-5-1

Contents

Contents

Not the Beginning

How that voice echoed in the emptiness. But that was long ago. Even then, it was long ago.

* * *

I know of a seagull called Widefaring. He flies far and wide. And every day he returns to perch on top of a tall pole that stands by the seashore in the south. Anyone who stands beneath that pole may have his wisdom dropped on them from above.

Widefaring says: "How things have changed, I never thought it would come to this!"

I know of a hawk called Farseer. He rarely flies at all, but every day he sits on top of a high fell. That fell is called Tower. Long ago, giants piled great rocks on top of that fell to raise it higher. And on the very top is another pile of smaller stones. Farseer sits on top of the pile of stones on top of the fell, and he sees as far as he can see.

Farseer says: "I never saw any bird called Widefaring fly this way. Widefaring flies far along the paths he knows, but he sees little."

Widefaring says: "Tower fell is often covered in cloud, and Farseer misses much. There are many valleys that he has never seen. And many of those valleys lie close to his high tower."

I know this: To speak to Farseer you must climb to the top of Tower fell, because Farseer will not fly down. The climb is difficult, and as you get near the top, many of the boulders will rock and move, and that part of the mountain is very unstable.

Widefaring says: "Why risk death? There are easier ways to come by knowledge about the world."

Farseer says: "And yet they come."

* * *

Farseer says: "How would you begin it?"

Widefaring says: "You are right to ask, though I never thought you would. One thing is certain: I would not begin at the beginning."

Farseer says: "That is hardly a surprise. Your ramblings lack direction and purpose. Who would listen?"

Two birds screamed on the mountaintop. A hawk sat on a stony perch. He ruffled his feathers and gazed into the far distance. Circling overhead, a seagull had flown far from the sea.

Widefaring says: "Little happened in the beginning. Who would want to listen to that? It is hardly a story to hear that nothing happened."

Farseer says: "How long was the world empty? Or what happened before the Elders came into the world, or before the men came? We all know what happened in the beginning. We all know how Skyrunner sang."

Widefaring says: "We all know that. But that is no way to tell the story. The story of Skyrunner can wait."

The Walls of Highgarth

Widefaring says: "Solway I saw, the witch on the northern coast. There she sat, watching the sea. I saw what happened next, but I don't suppose you saw it."

Farseer says: "I saw the movement in the water before she did, and I saw him come out of the sea. I see many things from the felltop where I sit. There is little point in flying around and around. Why would I waste my time? I saw what they did, Solway and that giant."

Widefaring says: "He didn't stay long with her, the sea giant. I was there. I saw it all with my own eyes. I am happy to fly across the wide world, there is little that I miss."

Farseer says: "I could see where he was headed long before he set off walking. I saw the Elders as they first stumbled into the old ruins that they now call Highgarth. They blundered around like babies, fighting and falling, seeing little and understanding less. It was a great wonder for them to find the old stone walls. I saw it all. I don't suppose you could discern anything from the distant blur if you were flying over the northern sea as you claim."

* * *

Solway the witch sat in the north. She sat on the seashore and gazed out across the water, just as Shoreguard sat in the south. She had been placed there, far-seeing, wide-watching, skilled in magic. It was not quiet there. Wavelets and ripples shuffled at the water's edge, and the wind conjured up noise out of nothing. Flocks of geese padded on the muddy banks where the river ran out into the sea.

3

Solway faced the north and watched the water. There was another land there, across the sea. Solway had never been to that land, but from all she could see of it, it looked rather similar to the place where she sat. It was as though she was looking into a great mirror. The young moon raised her head and she ran across the sky, and down below, the sea saw her running, and it flowed and followed as far as it could. The sea ran up to Solway's ankles, wet by the lapping of wavelets.

Solway the seer sat in the north and looked out across the water. That was when she saw a giant emerge from the depths and wade out onto the land.

"What is your name?" Solway asked him. "Or where have you come from?"

"I didn't come here to tell you my name," the giant said.

Solway thought about her horn. Perhaps if she had blown her horn then, Heave would have come running, and things would have turned out differently. But at that moment Solway did not know how things would go, and she didn't blow the horn.

"I have come a long way, and I still have far to go," said the giant. "But can I stay here tonight?"

And Solway said he could.

The giant didn't stay long in that place. When morning came, he was already away, walking inland, heading for the place they call Highgarth. And Solway was left alone again, watching the sea.

* * *

In a sheltered valley in the high mountains there is a certain spot. The Elders were filled with wonder when they found it, and they decided to make it their own. This place was protected on all sides by impassable slopes and high tops. There was only one way into that place, along a narrow, winding, and steep-sided valley. The upper end of that valley widened out, and the valley bottom there was flat and dry, warm and comfortable. But there was something else about that place: there were walls there. Old stone walls. The Elders could not have built such walls themselves, and they marvelled when they saw them. "These walls are the work of giants," they said. The walls, though, were in a state of disrepair. If this place had been occupied before, it must have stood empty for a long time. Some parts of the walls had fallen down, and it seemed as though some parts had been deliberately removed.

Hunter said: "This is a good place, and we should claim it as our own, but how can we live here?"

Blossom said: "We cannot simply sit under rocks like trolls or sleep in trees like wild men. It was good to find this place, but so much building work needs to be done."

Herder said: "It is easy to talk about building, but harder to do it."

Fairhair said: "A strong man would be able to raise these walls again to what they once were."

Heave said: "These stones are easy for me to lift. You would not know how to put the stones together. You could not build anything!"

Many of them had a good deal more to say on the subject, but the stones stayed still on the ground where they had fallen.

* * *

The giant walked for days. He crossed over a wide plain that lay beside the sea, and soon he was heading into the mountains that rose up in front of him. Even when he was with Solway he had been able to see those mountains. When they were far away, they had seemed a distant blue, but now the mountains became more real, and the colours changed to green and brown, yellow and grey. Little hills became bigger hills, and soon there were hills behind him as well as ahead, and rocky peaks towered high above the valley bottoms.

The giant walked along long lakes, and passed through wooded valleys. He climbed up towards mountain passes and passed teardrop tarns. There were animals there. Golden sheep grazed, and little birds chattered in the trees and flew up into the air as he passed by. In those days, there were few monsters or dangers in the world, or few things that could threaten a giant.

At last he reached the place where the hidden valley was. He turned into that valley, and he followed it up until he came to the place called Highgarth.

* * *

The Elders were still sitting among the ruined walls, some of them were still arguing about what to do. Others were asleep. But they soon woke up when the tall figure of the giant appeared, boldly walking up the valley. The Elders were shocked to see him approach, and they all sprang to their feet.

It was Mindrace who spoke first: "Tell me, who are you, or where have you come from?"

The giant said: "I didn't come here to tell you my name. I have come a long way to reach you here. I can see that you need a builder to repair these old walls, and to raise up halls. I can build these walls for you."

Mindrace said: "Tell me then, why have you come here to work?"

The giant said: "Why are you asking this? Are you not pleased that someone has come and offered to do this work for you? Or are there other builders who have come here to help you?"

Mindrace said: "It is often better to try to understand someone who says they come with something to offer. But I see my question was too broad. Tell me this then: why do you want to work, or what makes you want to build?"

The giant said: "I will answer this, but you ask a lot of questions. I have learned many things about building, and I have the skills to do it well. I have become a master builder. It would be careless for me not to use the talents I have, and to slowly forget everything I have learned. I suppose it is the same for all of us, that we want to leave our mark on the world, as best we can."

Mindrace said: "You say you have the skills to build a wall. But tell me then, why have you come here to us?"

The giant said: "I will answer this, but you ask a lot of questions. I heard that you had found this place. It is a special place that you have found here, but it is not in a good state. I know I can give you the help you need to improve this place, and to make it into what it can become."

Mindrace said: "These are interesting reasons, but this is not the whole story. Tell me, what do you want, or why do you think you will get it by working here?"

The giant said: "You are right to ask this. I can give you what you want, but you should also give me something in return. You must reward me fairly for my work. I will not ask for more than this, but also I will take no less."

Mindrace said: "Tell me then, what have you done before, or what made you leave your old work behind to come here?"

The giant said: "I have built walls before. I have built many walls. But you will have to take my word for that. I can see that no-one here could know how to approach the building of walls, and as I walked here I didn't pass any other builders who were on their way to help you. You ask a lot of questions, but you seem reluctant to accept the help you need."

Mindrace said: "It is this simple: I have to understand why someone would come here offering to help. Tell me this then: how do you see this going for you, or what do you think the future holds for you?"

The giant said: "It is difficult for me to see the future. Some might say that they can see it, but I cannot. And neither have I thought too long about how the future might look for me. It is better to live in the moment we are alive. I will make the future as good as I can for myself, but there will always be things I cannot control. You ask a lot of questions."

Mindrace said: "And yet still you stand here answering."

The giant said: "I came a long way to do this work. You should know I would rather get on with building than stand here answering questions."

Mindrace said: "Tell me this then: do you have any questions for us?"

The giant said: "I have many questions, and I expect they will all be answered, not by what you tell me now, but by what happens next."

Mindrace said: "Very well, I see you have decided that you will build these walls, and I don't think anyone here would object to that."

And so the giant began to work.

* * *

7

Widefaring says: "I saw that giant, fetching stones, carrying, cutting, carving. I saw him putting stones on top of stones. I don't suppose you saw it."

Farseer says: "I saw the walls taking shape. I saw them slowly grow, and I saw them become real where once they were only imagined. I see more things than you could understand. Why would I waste my time flying around when I can see so much without leaving my perch?"

Widefaring says: "I saw the Elders there in the middle of it all. They saw everything the giant was doing, but they understood nothing. They didn't watch, they didn't learn, they only marvelled at what was appearing before them. I was there. It was easy for me to see everything that happened."

Farseer says: "Mindrace I saw, walking by the walls, from hall to hall, wondering at what the giant had built. He was pleased with what he saw, but he knew then that he would have a problem paying this giant for the work."

Widefaring says: "Far I flew, further than you thought. There were other things happening in other places. I don't suppose you saw these things."

Farseer says: "Why would I fly? I saw what was happening in the north. I saw Solway sitting, swollen, expecting. I saw the water move."

* * *

While all this was going on, Solway sat in the north. There was something else about Solway the witch: ever since the giant had visited her, she had been growing more and more pregnant.

Solway was sitting, looking out across the water, when all at once she saw something move. It was some way out to sea, but it was coming closer. It was not long before a giantess stepped out of the sea and onto the shore.

Solway said to the giantess: "What is your name? Or where have you come from?"

"I could ask you your own name," the giantess said. "I came here looking for my husband, Finn. I could ask you whether you have seen him, or which way he went."

Solway said: "How would I know this? Or how could I know who your husband is? I never heard anyone speak that name."

The giantess said: "There can not be many giants who walk out of the sea. But I know he has been here because I can see he left something here with you. Or when is that baby due?"

"If Finn was that giant's name, I never knew it," said Solway. "If he was your husband, he didn't tell me that. And if he knew where he was headed, then that was something else he didn't tell me."

The giantess said: "Many deeds are done without a full knowledge of the facts. And many actions will have consequences later. Unintended results cannot always be foreseen."

And so the sea giantess strode away from the sea and headed inland. She walked away across the plain and towards the mountains where the giant had gone. And once again Solway sat alone on the shore.

* * *

The giant worked hard on the walls, and little by little they rose. The outer wall took shape, and the walls of the inner halls, and then rooves were put onto them. And so the work was finished, and the walls of Highgarth were built. And Highgarth stood like no other building in the world, strong and stable. It was a sight to see. The walls seemed impenetrable, and they would surely stand up to any attack by giants or trolls or any other creatures who might come there with bad intentions. And if there was a weak point in those walls, the Elders could not find it. It was generally agreed that the giant had done a good job.

And so the giant went to Mindrace to ask for his payment.

Mindrace said: "To build for the glory of Highgarth is reward enough. Your works will stand as your legacy. They are built in stone and they will last longer than you or I. When we are gone, the walls will remain, and men will say: these walls are the work of giants, we will never see their like again."

Then the giant said: "But is it not right that you should give me my reward for the work I have done for you? For my labour, or for the skills I have put to use?"

9

Mindrace said: "This place is our stronghold. There are those among us who could easily strike you down. It is easy for us to attack, and hard for you to defend yourself. You chose to walk in here alone. You should be grateful for the mercy you receive when we allow you leave this place in safety.

The giant said: "I will take two jewels from you. The brightest and most precious that you have. And this will be payment for the work."

Mindrace said: "I know of two jewels that shine brighter than any other. You also know them both. These two are the greatest treasures, and there is none greater. But what would you do if you possessed either of the two great treasures? The two jewels you asked for are the sun and the moon, for they are the brightest jewels in the sky. You may collect your payment whenever you want."

The giant said: "The sun and the moon are the most precious jewels in the sky. But I already have as much use as I might get from either of these two treasures, whether I own them or not. There are other treasures that I would rather own. The sun and the moon serve all who live on the land, and they are not yours to give."

Mindrace said: "If you demand the sun and the moon as payment, I say this: you may collect your payment whenever you want."

The giant said: "The sun and the moon are not the two jewels I will take. I will return later to claim what is mine."

And the giant walked back the way he had come. And the walls of Highgarth shone in the evening sunlight, and the moon rose over the mountain.

* * *

Solway the seer sat on the seashore. Her child was there beside her. She gazed northwards, but she felt the giant's footsteps approach as he crossed the plain.

And Solway called out to the giant: "Welcome back Finn, here to me. And what have you brought for your son to play with?"

As soon as the giant heard Solway speak his name, he stopped, stunned, and he was filled with rage.

The giant lifted up the baby boy, and he said: "If I left this child here with you, I see it was a mistake. And now I will be glad to correct it."

And the giant strode back into the sea, and he carried the baby boy with him. And the two of them disappeared beneath the waves.

* * *

Widefaring says: "Solway I saw, sitting on the seashore, alone again. I don't suppose you saw it."

Farseer says: "You can hardly imagine how much I see. I look around me, I use my eyes to watch the world. There is little point in wasting time and energy in flight. I have found a good place to sit. Yes, I saw her. The giant gone, the child gone. I saw her looking north, out to sea, watching the way he had come and the way they had gone."

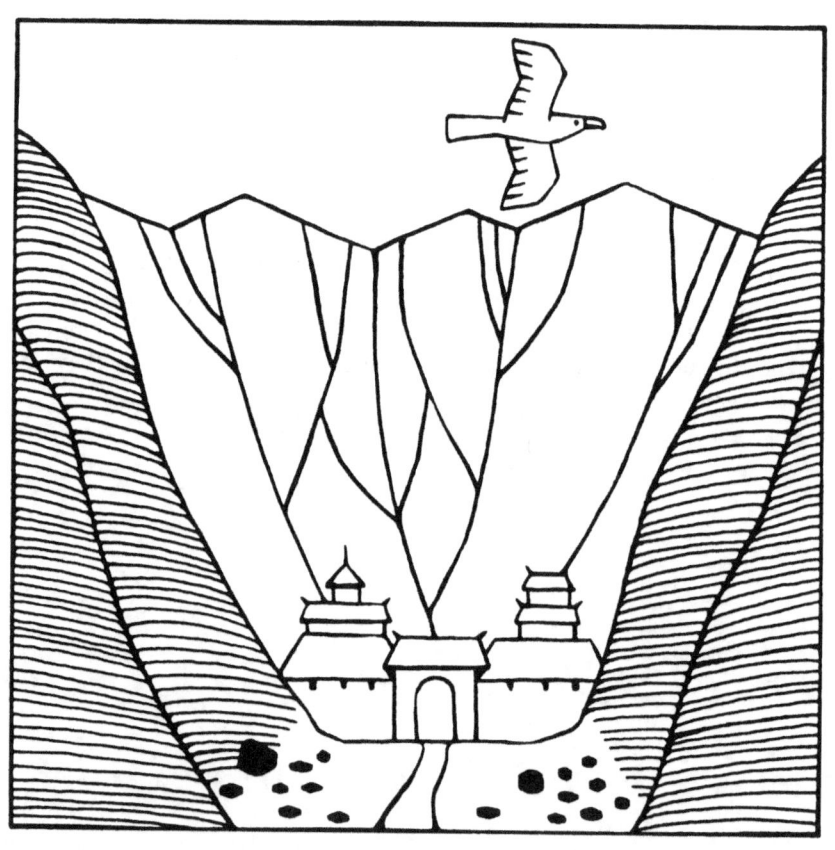

Memory and Imagination

I heard about a dwarf once, and I knew that I would have to find him. That dwarf was a long way below the earth. Many were the tunnels I followed, winding down, further and deeper into the earth. Dwarfs had made those tunnels. It is hard to imagine why dwarfs dig in the earth. That is one of the great mysteries. I followed on in the darkness. Many had walked that way before. At last I found the dwarf they call Imagination. They say that that dwarf is blind.

The dwarf says: "All the world is in my mind. It is just as I imagine it. I am hardly bothered by the darkness so far below the earth. I am hardly bothered by the blindness of my eyes. All the world is just as I see it.

"Many men come this way to ask me about my vision of the world. They must think it is worth the journey, to come into the depths to find me here. They must think I have something to offer them, more than the power of their own eyes."

* * *

Tell me then, who was it who killed Imagination. Who was it who slew that dwarf?

I saw the wolf come sneaking when the dwarf was walking. Sharp tooth, strong jaw. That wolf was hiding in the shadows, but it was always there. Long tongue, close face, hot breath, hard tooth. The wolf was real enough. The dwarf did not survive that attack. The wolf Reality has a strong bite, and it knows no mercy.

* * *

13

I know of a dwarf. I went to see him once. It is difficult to forget what happened that day, but it is also difficult to remember. It was unlike anything I had seen in the world. But if I had not seen the world, I hardly think I would have been able to find that dwarf.

The dwarf says: "Imagine you could understand the language of birds."

"Many men try to think what it would be like to fly. They see that birds can fly. All kinds of birds can do it, blue tits, buzzards, pheasants, owls. Ravens fly, sparrows fly, hawks fly, seagulls fly."

"In the sky it is easy to enter into a cloud. Many things seem different there. Some things are not as clear as they once were."

The dwarf says: "Look at things from another point of view."

"If you leave your body behind, climb higher into the air and soar, what will you see when you look behind? How will you see yourself from above?"

The dwarf says: "Things do not have to be the same as they always were."

"Paint a picture in your mind, think about what you can make in the world."

That dwarf was difficult to reach. He was higher than any other dwarf I ever saw. He was hidden in clouds. I had to fly to reach him. I had to find my way through a shroud of mist. I still don't know whether that dwarf was real, but I remember what he told me.

* * *

I know of another dwarf. I met him once. I went deep into the earth to find him. There were mines there, tunnels and underground ways. Dwarfs had made those. All around me, I could see the signs that dwarfs had been there before me. When I found that dwarf, I didn't ask him why dwarfs dug so deep into the earth. That was not why I had come there. I had heard he was there, and I came to speak to him about another matter. That dwarf was called Memory.

The dwarf says: "I have heard about those birds and the stories they tell. They say they have seen many things, and I am sure this is true. But there is a good reason men like to listen to those birds, and it is this: those birds have learned over many years how to tell a good story.

"I remember well when the earth was young, and Farseer told Mindrace the story of Skyrunner. I am sure that bird saw it all. But I remember how that same bird told the same story to a young hero who climbed the mountain only a month ago. Some parts of the story were passed over. The bird lingered longer over other parts of that story.

"A master storyteller will find out in the telling what his listeners like to hear. And those listeners will return again and again to hear the stories told. And with retelling after retelling, some parts of those stories will be spun out and rewoven. Memories become memories of memories. It may even be that memories of stories become memories themselves. All this I remember well."

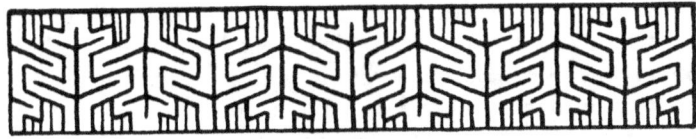

A Small Stone

Many days begin the same way in Oakdale: with a little light rain on the high canopy of oak leaves in the old woods, and Heave, the master of the hall at Oakdale, worrying about his daughter.

And what does a father worry about regarding his daughter? The great worry: the question of finding a suitable match. Finding a match is one thing. But suitability is quite another. The girl Heft was exceptional in beauty and size, and she had started to attract the attention of potential suitors. Most worryingly, it seemed that the rumours of her beauty had reached the land of the giants.

Heave said: "There is no need for me to use dragons or bears to protect my daughter. I know my own strength, and I am well capable of protecting her myself."

Heft laughed. "I too know my own strength," she said. "And I hardly need protecting from any man who might come this way."

But Heave had decided that he would have to visit the mountains in the north to teach the giants a thing or two. He would teach them about staying away from his daughter. And he would teach them using his swinging club.

* * *

So Heave set off walking. The path led down through the woods of upper Oakdale towards the lake Overwater. Beyond that lake lay the mountains where he thought he would find the giants.

As Heave was walking, he saw a small stone on the path in front of him. Sometimes when he saw small stones on the path, he would kick them with his foot into the long grass that grew alongside. It was good to keep the paths clear of such obstructions. Though in all honesty, such a small stone on a path could hardly be called an obstruction. Such a small stone could be easily ignored. There was plenty of room to place a foot (or indeed both feet) on either side of the small stone and walk on by. Or it would be easy to step on the small stone, pressing it into the mud, and then continue along the way. There would probably be other small stones on the path ahead, and one thing was certain: the giants that walked in chaos through the mountains were a lot bigger and a lot more interesting than a small stone.

He hardly thought about it as he swung his club at the stone, meaning to clear it from the path and send it some distance away. The club struck true, but the small stone didn't move.

Heave had hardly checked his pace when he swung at the stone. But now he stopped, surprised, and looked again. The small stone lay still on the path. He raised his club and he swung it again. He struck the stone, but the stone didn't move. And when Heave looked at the stone and saw it still lying on the path, he noticed a strange thing. It was almost as though the small stone was a little bigger than it had been. It was almost as though it had grown.

Heave knew that he would have to shift the stone from the path, and that the way to do it was by the force of his swinging club. With this club, he had struck and shattered the bones of many giants, and there was no doubt in his mind that with this same club he should be able to easily remove a small stone from a path. So he swung again, and he struck the stone. But it didn't move. And when he looked at the stone where it lay still on the path, there could now be no doubt. The stone was definitely bigger than it had been.

He struck the stone again and again. It didn't move, but it grew and grew until it was almost as high as Heave himself, and so wide that it was completely blocking the path.

By now Heave was furious. He cried out as he swung his club. It smashed into the side of the stone. This was no longer a small stone. Now it was a boulder, growing bigger with every strike. Heave had forgotten all about the giants north of Overwater. His whole mind and his whole being was occupied with the thought of clearing the path. He struck the stone again and again. But the stone stayed still.

At last, Heave grew tired. And with all thoughts forgotten of why he had gone out in the first place, he turned back. He left what was now a great boulder behind him, and he returned home to his hall in Oakdale.

* * *

There was a great storm that day. The trees shook and the heavens flashed. The clouds in the sky trembled, and rain fell over the whole country. Craggy mountain faces glistened wet under their cloudy hoods. The water rushed down the mountains in swollen streams, crashing and tumbling through the rocks, as white as milk. And the water reached the lakes, and the lakes filled as far as they could, and it was not far enough, and they filled up further and the water spilled out into the surrounding land. And all that time, the great boulder stayed quite still. And when the rain had stopped and the lake waters had slowly retreated back to their usual boundaries, the great boulder was completely blocking the place where the path had been. So Heave had to find a new path and a longer way so that he didn't have to pass by that boulder as he went down the valley.

The Myth of Luck

The girl shivered on the mountaintop. She pulled her cloak closer around her where she was crouched, and she leaned in to where the bird was sitting so that she could hear what it said.

"Tell me," said the girl. "How is it that Mindrace is the chief and leader of the Elders?"

"That is simple to answer: Mindrace is lucky. All he has, he got through luck, and without luck, he would have none of it."

"Tell me then, how is Mindrace so lucky?"

"That is easy to explain. Mindrace is lucky because he holds the stone called Luck. As long as he holds that stone, his luck will endure. Few dare to challenge him, as they fear they would lose to the luckier man. But if he should lose the stone, he may find that things do not go well for him after that."

"Tell me then, how did Mindrace get the stone called Luck?"

"I will tell you how it happened," said the bird. And the bird told this story:

Long ago, Mindrace was sitting in the high seat in Highgarth, when a red-headed boy came to speak to him.

"I have heard of a certain stone," said the boy. "That stone is called Luck, and it will bring good luck to anyone who holds it. If you were to get that stone, it could bring you easy victories in battle, and you could live a comfortable life. Few would dare to challenge you. It would be good for you to have that stone. Why don't you go and take it?"

"That stone would be good to have," said Mindrace. "But I don't know where I might find it. And if someone already has the stone, I imagine it might be difficult to take it from them, as luck would be on their side."

The boy said: "Luck is well hidden, and is not easy to find. The stone is hidden under water. A giant sits nearby keeping watch. They say that that giant never sleeps, and that his head is as hard as stone. To reach that giant, you must pass through a land that is watched over by a flying dragon. It will not be easy to reach the place where the stone is without attracting the attention of that dragon. The stone is hard to find, but if you find it, it will be easy for you to take it. They don't know what they have, and they will not miss it until it is gone."

* * *

North of Highgarth, among the high fells, there is a deep valley, and in the bottom of that valley there is a lake, long and dark. The valley is crooked and winding, so it is impossible to see from one end of the lake to the other. On both sides of the water, the mountains rise steeply, and the lower parts of those slopes are strewn with stones and great boulders that were flung across the valley by giants long ago. The fishermen on that lake tell stories about another creature that lies hidden beneath the dark water. There is a waterfall there called High Force. The water falls all the way from the high plateau down to the valley bottom. The roar of that waterfall can often be heard from far away, but the waterfall itself is almost hidden by tall trees. Anyone wanting to see that waterfall would have to come very close, walking through the trees, and crossing over wet and slippery rocks.

The northern fells lie beyond that lake, but between the lake and those fells there is an area of wilderness that must be crossed. That place is filled with marshes, and some parts are covered in trees. It is difficult to see very far, and easy to get lost in the woods. There are two rivers that flow through that district, and any traveller who failed to find the right way would have to cross one or both of those rivers.

Mindrace picked his way along the edge of the dark waters of the lake as waves blew in and splashed against the boulders on the shoreline. The light that reached down into the valley was pale, and the sky had just started to become red. The grey man could hardly be seen among the rocks. Mindrace knew that he was coming closer to places where dragons might be seen of an evening, high in the air above the highest felltops. But as he looked up, he saw none.

A dwarf was sitting by the lake shore, close to the place where the stream from High Force runs into the water.

"I need to reach the northern fells," Mindrace said to the dwarf. "Will you tell me how I can get there?"

"I can easily tell you the way," said the dwarf. "But that place is the domain of giants, watched over by flying dragons. It might be foolish for you to try to go there."

"I am not so afraid of dragons or giants," said Mindrace. "In fact, they may be able to help me more easily find what I am looking for.

The dwarf didn't speak, but Mindrace went on: "You are probably wondering what I am looking for. I have come here to find a certain stone called Luck. I have heard that the one who holds this stone will become lucky."

"Why would you need such a stone?" said the dwarf. "You already sit in the high seat at Highgarth. You are already comfortable in your position. The Elders think of you as their chief and leader."

"If I held this stone, I would never have to worry about anything again," Mindrace said.

The dwarf said: "If you walk north from here in a straight line, you will surely come to the place where you are going."

Mindrace said: "It will be difficult to keep a straight line in an area filled with marshes and woods."

"I cannot tell you more than I have already told you," said the dwarf. "I have already given you my best advice."

So Mindrace set off. I will not spend too long telling how Mindrace crossed that area of wilderness, but it took him rather longer than he had hoped. It is not easy to walk in a straight line through a marsh: the ground is often soft and unstable, and the way ahead may be blocked by patches of open water. In open land, when the way ahead can be seen, it is easier to deviate to find firmer footing, and it is easier to continue in the right direction. In the woods, more things may block the way, fallen trees, dense undergrowth, and without a clear view, it can be hard to get back on track after a deviation. Mindrace didn't find a path through that wild area, and he wandered for a long time while clumps of rushes grabbed at his feet and dragged him down into the wet ground.

At last, he reached the other side. The land rose higher, the ground grew drier, and the trees grew sparse. And before long, he could look back and see all the way across that place where he had walked.

The ground rose steeply, and Mindrace climbed higher. And when he came over a ridge, he saw before him a great hollow in the mountainside, enclosed on three sides by rocky mountain walls, steep and high. In the bottom of the hollow there was a tarn. A stream flowed out from the mouth of the tarn. It dropped steeply at first, chattering and tumbling over rocks. Then it reached a valley that wound its way down the mountain and out of sight. Above the still water of the tarn, Mindrace could see a cloud of mist, and as he looked closer, he saw in the cloud a dragon that had come to the water's edge to drink. Steam was rising into the chilly air where the dragon lay. Mindrace approached the dragon, and it raised its head, its eye glinting gold.

Mindrace said to the dragon: "Tell me, dragon with the gleaming eye: what is this place, or who are you who lies drinking at the lakeshore?"

The dragon said: "It is hardly right to ask someone's name without revealing who you are yourself. Who are you who comes here walking? This is a place I come to every day. I suppose anyone I might meet here would know who I was, but I have never seen you here before."

Mindrace said: "I have come a long way to reach this place. I thought I would find a dragon here. They call me Grey. I am surprised you didn't know this already. Perhaps you don't know as much as you thought."

The dragon said: "Who dares to enter this country knowing that there is a dragon here? Did you think you would come here unnoticed? Did you think you would pass by me unseen? I suppose you thought you would find something else here as well. Did you think you could come here and find my golden hoard? It will not go well for you if you try to take it."

Mindrace said: "There is little point in trying to hide it: I did come here looking for something. Though I don't suppose it is something you have, or something you value. I don't suppose it is even made of gold. Tell me then: is your treasure hidden under this very tarn?"

The dragon said: "It is hardly right to ask a dragon where its den is, or where its treasure is hidden. But I have no reason to keep this a secret from you as you will not manage to take the treasure. If you knew as much about dragons as you claim, you would know this already: the treasure is not kept under water. Rather it is hidden under the hill. Many men have come here. Most thought that they would leave with more than they came with. But the men that left this place all took away less than they brought. Others didn't leave at all."

Mindrace said: "There is still one thing I want from you. But it is not from your hoard."

The dragon said: "You may ask for whatever you want. But I don't suppose you will get it."

Mindrace said: "I have heard there is a giant in this country, or a troll. He sits by the water. I can see no giant next to this tarn, but you might tell me if you have seen where the giant sits."

The dragon said: "I have no reason to hide it from you. But I have no reason to tell you where you might find the troll. It is not difficult to see that the only river that flows on this mountain is the beck that flows out of this tarn. I have already told that troll that you are coming, so he will be expecting you."

Mindrace said: "How have you done that, as I have not seen you leave this place?"

The dragon said: "I have been watching you for some time. I saw you when you wandered, lost on Bleaberry Moss. I saw the roundabout route you took as you blundered through the birch trees. It was before you saw me here at the tarn, that's when I told the troll you were coming."

Mindrace left the dragon behind, and he followed the beck down from the tarn.

Many valleys are shaped as though they had been scraped out of the mountain by a huge spoon. But this valley was not like that. It was as though a great blade had cut into the smooth mountainside, leaving a deep wound. The stony beck trickled and tumbled in the bottom of that valley. Mindrace soon reached a small waterfall and a pool, and by the side of the pool, a giant was sitting, still as a stone.

"I have been expecting you," said the giant. "I heard that an old man was coming this way, grey as the clouds in the sky."

Mindrace said: "I have come a long way to find this place, and here you sit, just as I thought."

The giant said: "I see a wanderer who has come walking into a place he doesn't know. I think you have come searching for something. Tell me what you want, and I will help you if I can."

Mindrace said: "I am searching for something. There is no reason to deny it. If I told you I was not searching for anything you would hardly believe me."

The giant said: "If you have come here searching for a great treasure, you may be disappointed. There is no magic here. I am not guarding anything, as you may have been told."

Mindrace said: "It is difficult to believe that you are not guarding something here, or that you sit and keep watch for no reason on this desolate fellside far from anywhere."

The giant said: "I am happy enough here. You may call this place the edge of the world, but there is no reason for me to be dissatisfied. This place is the centre of the world for me, and I already have all I could want."

Mindrace said: "If you are happy it is because you hold that one magic stone, and you guard it carefully."

The giant said: "You have come here to find something, and I will try to help you. I came to this place to live a satisfied life. Perhaps that is itself a great treasure. I cannot say whether or not it is a secret, but there is no great magic to it."

Mindrace had to decide what to do. And before long, he had decided.

The stream that flowed there was called Stoneybeck. Mindrace put his hand into the water and pulled out a stone from the bed of the stream. He held the stone up, and he spoke these words:

"This stone is called Luck. I found it in the river. A dragon guarded it and it didn't know what it was guarding. A giant watched over it, but he didn't know what he had in his possession."

Mindrace took the stone back to Highgarth. He called all the Elders before him, and he showed them the stone: "I have found

Luck. It would be unwise to challenge me while I have this stone in my possession. This is surely one of the greatest treasures of this land, and I feel very lucky to have it."

Mindrace held onto that stone for a long time after that, and for as long as he had it, it brought him a lot of luck.

The Ram Raid

While Mindrace was out walking one day along the seashore, where the waves rolled in and rattled the shingle around his feet, he saw something floating in the water.

He waded out, and when he reached it, he saw that it was a basket, coated in tar, that had drifted in on the tide. And lying in the basket was a small red-haired boy.

"Who are you, or how did you get here?" Mindrace asked the boy.

But the boy didn't answer, because he didn't know how to speak.

"I will call you Robin," said Mindrace, "for your red hair."

And Mindrace took the boy back with him to Highgarth.

That boy grew up quickly, and soon he could speak well enough. Though there were many who wished he had never learned.

* * *

There was a farmer called Fisher, and the farm where he lived was called Newgrange. This farmer had a ram called Goldwool. The ram had been a gift from a dwarf, and it was a magical ram. The ram had a golden fleece, and every year its wool would be shorn off. The shorn wool was all of pure gold, but the ram would grow more, and the next year it would be shorn again. Robin knew this, and he said to Herder: "This ram would be good for you to have in your own flock. And you may also see whether any lambs born to this ram would have golden fleeces of their own."

Herder said: "That ram may be good to own, but it may not be easy to take it."

Robin said: "Come with me, and we will get the ram together."

So Robin and Herder dressed themselves as fiddlers. They put on musicians' clothes. Herder took a fiddle, and Robin took some bells, and they went to Fisher's farm at Newgrange.

It happened that there was a feast taking place in that hall. So Herder played and Robin sang, and they kept everyone well entertained. They played the song about the great warrior Blue, and the song about the farmer and the crow, and the song about the Grange duck raid. And they also played many more songs and many tunes.

After a while, most of the guests grew tired from drinking and dancing, and they collapsed onto the floor and slept.

The next day, Fisher came to the two musicians. He told them that he was so pleased with their singing and playing that he would give them a gift of their choice.

"We would very much like to have the ram Goldwool," said Robin.

"Alas that cannot be," said Fisher. "That ram was given to me by the dwarf Oldrich on the condition that I would never give it away."

"That is a great shame," said Robin. "But in that case, perhaps you would allow us to buy the ram from you."

"No," said Fisher. "That cannot be. I also promised the dwarf Oldrich when he gave me the ram that I would never sell it."

None of this was a surprise to Robin, as he already knew these things.

"That is a shame," he said. "We saw that ram as we walked here, and I must say I was very taken with the idea of owning it. But if it can't be given away as a reward, and it can't be bought, perhaps there is a way that I could tempt you to part with the ram in a way that would not cause you to go back on the agreement you made with the dwarf. What would you say about an exchange? The dwarf Oldrich surely didn't forbid this as well?"

"Yes, you are right," Fisher said. "Oldrich did not say anything about an exchange. But tell me what you two fiddlers could have that I might want to exchange for Goldwool."

"I will show you what we have," said Robin, "but you will have to wait here while we go and fetch it."

Fisher agreed, and Robin and Herder walked away into the woods that surrounded Fisher's farm. The ash and birch trees were widely spaced, and the spring sunshine shone down, touching the green leaves that were growing on the woodland floor. There were silver snowdrops there, and golden daffodils. Some of those flowers grew taller than the others that surrounded them, and Robin hit those flowers with his stick as he walked past so that their heads flew off.

"What are you looking for?" asked Herder. "Or what are you going to give him?"

"I am looking for a mushroom," said Robin.

"I don't think he will think much of a mushroom," said Herder.

"I think when he sees it, he will like it very much," said Robin.

There was a clearing in the woods, and they found a mushroom growing there. Robin spoke certain words over that mushroom, and it was transformed at once into a magnificent horse. The horse was dapple-grey with a dark mane. Robin led the horse back through the woods to the farm, and he showed the horse to Fisher.

"I suppose you have never seen a horse quite like this one before," he said. "I have owned this horse since the day it came into the world, but I will exchange it now for the ram, if you agree."

And Fisher agreed, so Robin and Herder left with the ram.

It was a pity for Fisher, though, that the magic didn't last for long. When he went to the stable the next day to look at the horse, all he saw was a mushroom lying on the stable floor. He knew then that he had been robbed, and he knew who it was who had been visiting him.

Redstone the Dwarf

Under the mountains there are many dwarfs. Those dwarfs work together every day, and they make many things from what they find in the earth. Every day, they dig and smith and forge. Hammers and axes are swung, bellows are pumped, and goods are loaded. And with all this work, songs are sung.

I know of a town called Fellfoot. That town lies at the foot of the fell, where the slopes of a high mountain drop to the lake shore. These are some of the dwarfs that are under that mountain: Clay, Gravel, Rubble, Delving, and Pit. I also know of other dwarfs in that mountain: Copperhead and Coppernick, Bluestone and Greengrey. There are many more.

There is a dwarfish hall under that mountain. The walls of that place are decorated in copper and other metals, cobalt and nickel. So although it is not as bright as the light of day under the mountain, it is a good deal lighter than you may think. The light that comes from glowing torches is not lost, but scattered and spread in shimmering reflections.

Some dwarfs work metal into fine-patterned objects, with bright and deep colours bound into them. Some carve stones with leaves and flowers and birds that are so real that they burst into life. Those dwarfs are skilled, and their talents are in high demand.

One time, one of the Elders was out walking on that mountain. There was a bird on top of the mountain, and people would often climb the mountain to speak to that bird. So there was a well-worn path up the mountainside.

It was the Lady Fairhair who was out walking. She reached her hand deep into the mountain, and she pulled out a dwarf.

Of course, the dwarf was not happy about this: "Put me down! Put me back! Who are you, or what do you want?" he shouted.

But Fairhair held on tight to the dwarf, and she lifted him up to her face so that she might see him well.

"Do you know who I am?" he asked her.

"No, I don't know that," Fairhair answered.

"My name is Redstone, and I am a dwarf," he said.

"I don't like that name at all," she said. "That sounds very common. Just the sort of name you might expect for a very plain thing that might be found on a mountainside. But you are not plain at all. You are very pretty. I mean to take you home with me and polish you up, and I imagine you will become prettier still. But that name will not do at all. I will call you Garnet."

And for all his objections, Redstone the dwarf had to admit he was a little curious about Fairhair who had pulled him out of the earth, and how she lived, and where, and how it would be to be polished and called by another name. To be called Garnet didn't sound such a terrible thing. So he relented, and he stopped struggling as Fairhair held him. Though as she set off down the mountain carrying the dwarf in her hand, he still had a scowl on his face.

Fairhair walked through the valleys, along the edge of a long lake, under the shadows of the high mountains. And soon she came to a large house surrounded by apple trees, all of them covered in white apple blossom. "This is Applegarth," she said to the dwarf. "This is my house. And this is where you will be staying. Here with me."

Fairhair showed Garnet (as she called him) where he would sleep on a fine feather bed. And she had all manner of fine food brought out, the like of which the dwarf had never seen or tasted, or even heard tell of. There were peacocks' eggs to eat, and the drink tasted like it had been squeezed from heather blossom.

The next morning, Fairhair said to the dwarf: "You should not have to suffer that hard life under the mountain. I will show you there is a better way to live.

"I would like you to give me advice on matters of style. You must know I am a great admirer of dwarfish design. I love the way all the elements of nature are included into those patterns – with the forms of branching trees, twisting leafwork, and breaking waves. Fur and feathers, fowl and deer. And the colours! The dwarfs have such a good eye for colour.

"Yes, you must advise me. But first, we must have new clothes made for you. These ones are so dirty with mud and grime. I will have my dressmakers sew new clothes for you at once.

"All in red," she said. "To match your fine name."

And so Garnet began his new life. He was surrounded by so many magnificent things. And Fairhair took him with her whenever she went travelling, and she introduced him to grand people dressed in fine clothes, all adorned in gold. And they all seemed delighted to meet him.

They all asked his opinion about matters that he had never even considered when he was living under the mountain, and they nodded thoughtfully whenever he spoke.

There was gold and jewellery equal to the best that he had seen under the mountain, but there was more than that. There were silks and furs and fine foods and delicate drinks. And the music was quite different from what he was used to. At times it was joyful, at times sorrowful, and at times it soothed him into a comfortable sleep.

He was enjoying life very much, and he hardly thought about the dwarfs he had left behind under the mountain at all. And so things went on for some time.

One day, Fairhair was sitting in the hall at Applegarth in the high seat, and Garnet was there with her. It was not a special day. There was nothing particularly out of the ordinary about that day. A fiddler was there, and he was singing songs. But it seemed that it would be a day when songs are sung, not a day that songs would be written about.

And then everything changed.

A great black crow flew in through the window and alighted on Fairhair's shoulder. The bird looked right at Garnet, and then it whispered something into Fairhair's ear.

Garnet could neither hear nor understand what the bird had said. But he sensed that it was about him. Fairhair didn't look at Garnet, but she whispered something back to the crow that Garnet did not hear, and then the bird flew back out the way it had come.

For a while after that, things seemed to be carrying on at Applegarth as before. No-one said anything to Garnet, but he could sense that something had changed. There were whispers. Rooms went quiet when Garnet walked in. Glances were cast in Garnet's direction when people thought he was looking the other way. The worst was that he could not guess what everyone might be whispering about. Of course, it must be something about him, but he could not guess what.

A little time later, Fairhair came to speak to Garnet: "I am going to spend some time at Highgarth," she said.

"Oh, how wonderful," Garnet said. He tried to speak as though nothing was wrong. "I have actually been thinking about what you might wear for this trip ..."

But Fairhair stopped him. "You won't be coming this time," she said. "And what is more, I expect that you will have gone by the time I get back."

Garnet stood and watched Fairhair and her party go until they disappeared behind some trees. Behind him, the door to Applegarth closed, and he was left there alone.

Outside the hall in the wild world, things seemed very bad for the dwarf. Nothing seemed familiar. Although he had stood in this place many times before, it had always been with Fairhair. She had always been the reason he was there. She had always told him what to do. And she had always provided him with shelter from whatever unknown things might be hiding behind the next hill, or the next tree, or the next rock. Big black birds flew high overhead, and Garnet shivered.

He was not sure where to go, but he started walking in a direction he thought he knew.

Despite the dwarf's fears, very little happened to him for some time. He hardly saw another creature. There were rare occasions when he came close to a hare or a sheep, but they hardly seemed to notice he was there.

One time, Garnet saw a woman walking. She was dressed in fine clothes with many gold ornaments.

"I will stop to speak to this woman," thought Garnet. And as she reached him on the path, he began to speak: "I wonder ..." he said.

But the woman didn't pause for a moment. She just walked on by as though she saw him no different from any stone lying in the road.

"I hardly know how I will survive out here in the world," cried Garnet, "and no more do I know how I might find my way back to the mountain."

On he walked, for fifteen days and fifteen nights, and he grew so tired that he could hardly take another step. He lay down to rest, and he slept a long sleep. And as he lay sleeping, the dwarf dreamed about many things. He dreamed about Fairhair and his fine life at Applegarth. He dreamed about the place under the mountain where he had come from and where he hoped he might return. But most he dreamed about the black bird, and he worried and wondered what that bird might have whispered in Fairhair's ear.

After a long sleep he awoke, and as he looked around, the landscape seemed a little familiar. So he started walking, and sure enough, when he passed over the brow of a hill and descended through a short stretch of woodland, the view that met him was the outline of the mountain where he had grown up.

He was home.

Garnet shone as he walked down the tunnel into the mountain. He heard the old familiar sounds of metal on stone echoing towards him from the depths of the mountain. And there were the voices, the rhythm and tones of work songs filling out the clanking beat of hammers and axes. This was what he knew.

"It's Redstone," someone said.

"I have had such an adventure," Garnet said, and he told them all about it.

"Is he from here?" some of the younger dwarfs asked. They didn't know who Garnet was. "Why does he talk like that? I can hardly understand him."

"What is he wearing?" others asked. "Is he even a dwarf?"

"Yes, I am from here," said Garnet. "Once I was just the same as you."

"You were the same as us once," someone said. "But we are not the same now. I don't suppose you want to work. I don't suppose you want to get your hands dirty and ruffle your fine clothes. I suppose you would prefer to have everything brought to you while you sit around and decide this or that."

Garnet didn't try to teach the dwarfs his new name. They all called him Redstone, which he didn't like. He folded up his fine clothes, and he went to work, though he no longer enjoyed it. He hardly ever sang. Every day he thought about the good times at Applegarth. Sometimes he thought about the great black bird, and he tried to guess what it might have whispered. He guessed many different things, but he never knew whether or not he had guessed right. Or if he had guessed right, he never knew which of his guesses was the right one. The dwarf continued to live the life that had once been the only thing he knew. But now he was not satisfied. Now his heart was elsewhere. His greatest hope was that a hand would reach into the mountain once again and pull him out. But that never happened.

The Stablemates

I was young once. High was the hall where I lived, and deep was the mountain valley where it lay. That hall was built of great blocks of stone that could only have been put there by giants. But taller still were the mountain walls that rose high on both sides of that valley.

There was another young man who lived there, his name was Eldebrand, and he was my dear friend.

> I lived in a hall so wondrous high
> High were the halls of my home
> High were the walls the giants built
> Hewn from the hardest rock and stone
> The mountain walls of my home

* * *

One day we climbed together up the side of the valley until the walls of the high hall lay far below us. When we reached the crest of the ridge, we could see over to the other side, we could see all the places we knew, and it seemed that the whole world was stretched out before us.

> High I climbed with my brother in arms
> As high as we could be
> And far we gazed over all the world
> As far as we could see

> Far beyond our house and hall
> And anywhere we'd been
> We saw the edge of the world of men
> And all as far as the place at the end
> But not beyond the place at the end
> For that is still unseen

Eldebrand said: "How are things with you, or why did you want to climb up to this place?"

I said: "The truth is, I have been troubled for some time. I have dreamed a dream, and the same dream comes back to haunt me again and again."

> Last night, as I lay sleeping
> Last night, as I lay in my bed
> Visions came shining
> And figures were walking
> And dancing and talking
> As light and as bright as the day
> Though I lay all the night
> All alone in my bed
>
> A girl I saw in the darkness
> A girl who was shining so bright
> The glittering stars were all in her arms
> And she scattered the starry light

I said: "I never saw any girl like that in all the world."

Eldebrand said: "There is one girl I know who you should meet. But if you dare to go to her it may be the end of you."

I said: "Until now I have been happy to live in this world, I am surrounded by all that I know, and by everything that has brought me satisfaction. But now I feel that everything is ending. The time has come to go away. I am not afraid to follow my fate, or to go hunting far from home. If you know where this girl is to be found, I must go there, and I cannot rest until it is done."

* * *

When I told my mother that I would be going away, she said this: "For this errand, you will need certain things that you do not have. I will help you by giving you these gifts."

I said: "I will need a horse."

My mother said: "This horse is Lightfoot. He can run through the darkest night, and leap through flickering flame."

I said: "I will need a sword."

My mother said: "This sword is Dawnray. It will slay the worst monster, or clear the way if a troll should block your path."

I said: "I will need a key."

My mother said: "This key is Openness. It will open a locked door, and no gate will bar the way."

Then Eldebrand said: "Wear this ring. It will be more difficult for any monster to see you, and you will weigh less heavily on this horse's back when you ride with me."

We did not stay too long after that. My mother waited by the gate to watch as we rode away.

* * *

For days we rode, for fifteen days
We rode unceasing through that place
Through mist and rain and sunshine bright
For fifteen days and fifteen nights
We rode to the edge of the world

And so we reached the edge of the world
The edge of all we once had known
Ahead there lay a great divide
And far across to the other side
And far to fall below

The gap was filled with flickering flame
But the horse we rode, it showed no fear
The horse leapt on and further on
And the world behind was past and gone
It leapt across the gap so wide
And we came to land on the other side

And if we were safe in our landing in that strange country, there were many things there that reminded us that we should not be too comfortable. For as we rode, we passed by untold horrors.

On we rode and further on. We came to a river, and I longed to drink and bathe in the water, but to my horror I saw that the river ran red. It was not water, but blood that flowed in that stream. On we rode and further on. I saw an iron forest of false trees, leafless things as dark as lead. Below those forged and beaten trunks, scraps of tinsel lay, clinking as our feet fell. And on we rode and further on. I saw a wild beast running. A wolf moved silently across the heath. But few could mistake its intentions: it held in its mouth the arm of a man.

Each time I saw such an awful sight, I thought of the world we had left behind, and I said to Eldebrand: "Far have we come from the fair valley, and the high hall we call home. This is a grim place we have found. Better for us now to turn back."

But Eldebrand said: "Better to think less about going back. Times that are gone will never return. There is something here for you, and you may be glad to have it, though things seem bad now."

And so we rode on.

* * *

After some time, we came to a great plain, and sheep were grazing there. A herdsman sat on a hill. And behind the herdsman stood a great house, the gates were closed and locked.

"Stay quiet awhile," Eldebrand said to me. "I will talk to this herdsman."

> A herdsman still sat on a hill
> Watching his flocks on the fell
> Long were the days he watched the ways
> And few were those who escaped his gaze
> Or missed what he did tell
>
> What riders ride on the fell today?
> Who dares to come this way?
> Who dares to ride in the grey-green grass?
> For many ride, but none may pass

Who dares to ride this way today?
You're not a man, you're not an elf
Have you come here to die today?
Or are you dead, as I believed

I'm not a man, I'm not an elf
But do you not know what I am?
Or can you not see for yourself?
Or am I not what you believed?

Eldebrand said to the herdsman: "I am not dead, as you thought, and I have not come here to die. I have come here for the sake of the maiden who lives in the house. It is for the sake of Winterlong's daughter that I came here."

The herdsman said: "The gates are closed for you and you will find it hard to enter in. You will never go into that house to speak with Winterlong's daughter."

Eldebrand said: "You have missed who you are talking to. There is a good reason I came here, and if there is one thing I will do in my life, it will be to speak to this girl."

The herdsman said: "Many men have come here with one thing in mind. They thought they had lost their minds, but soon they lost their heads. They came here with blood flowing fast in their veins, but soon their blood was flowing free in the rivers of this land. So you boy, set your sword away, there are things for you here that are hard to slay."

* * *

Around the house was a wall so high
Too high for a horse to leap
And on the wall were dead men's heads
They'd dared to ride but failed before
They'd come and seen but saw no more
They faced the past with eyeless gaze
And never again would sleep

The gates were all of iron
The walls were all of stone
And round and round and round we rode
But there was no way in

Round and round and round we rode
Where many had rode before
Yet though the walls stood tall and firm
I held the key to the door

The locks and chains all fell away
The gates were opened wide
And like the sun at the end of the day
We quickly rode inside

* * *

Then Eldebrand let out a great cry. It was so loud that it even seemed to echo around that wide-open place. They must also have heard him in the house, as before too long, a maiden came running out. She was dressed in armour, with a sword held in her hand. The earth trembled under her as she ran.

The girl said: "Who are these madmen who stand screaming in the yard?"

When I saw her, I could no longer keep quiet. I said: "I am not a madman, as you thought, maiden. Or if I am mad, I was driven mad by the thought of you. The truth is, I came here for your sake."

She said: "If you came here for my sake, then what have you brought for me on your horse?"

I said: "This is a thing all warriors know: gold stays at home when riding to war, for the battlefield is no place for treasure."

Then the girl smiled. She said: "I have not been a good hostess. Guests who have travelled so far must be hungry and thirsty. Welcome to my home."

So the girl led us into the house, and she gave us water to drink.

But no sooner had we sat down at the table than she leapt up with her sword drawn, and she raised it above our heads. The only way out of that hall was blocked by the herdsman, who also stood with a sword drawn and raised.

"Things are not going as well for you as you thought they would," said the girl.

Then Eldebrand spoke, and he called the girl by her own name: "Grip," he said, "do you not know me?"

The girl said: "You know my name, but I don't know who you are. You found me here, but I didn't tell you the way. Is it true that you killed my brother? I am afraid that he is dead, and he would hardly have told you these things. What are you then? Not a man, not a dwarf, not an elf."

Eldebrand said again: "Do you not know me?"

But the girl didn't speak. She stood in fury, ready to bring that sword down on either one of us, or on each of us in turn.

Then Eldebrand said:

> Sister, sister, still your sword
> For this is the man that I have brought
> I have brought him here for you
> As I promised long ago

Then the girl said: "Is it really you, Eldebrand, come back here at last? Is this the warrior you brought here for me? Then it is good that you came."

Then the herdsman cried out: "It is the young master, come back to us after all this time."

And so Grip and I were married, and there was gladness and more delight as we all celebrated the wedding together there in Winterlong's house.

And that is how I met Grip. Things were very different for me after that.

The Myth of Skyrunner

How that voice echoed in the emptiness.

Skyrunner hung in the air when the world was empty, and nothing was all that there was. When Skyrunner started to sing, there was no-one there to hear. There was nowhere for anyone to be.

How long Skyrunner had prepared for this moment. How long he had spent sharpening and polishing his craft. How well he had learned the words to sing, and each of the melodies that belonged to each verse. How long he had listened and learned, all in preparation. And how he had longed for this moment when his performance would begin.

So Skyrunner sang, and everything he sang came to be.

Skyrunner sang of the sea and the sky. He sang about the two sisters, so alike, reflecting each other's moods. He sang about the depths of their blue faces on a fair day, and he sang about the clouds and the waves. He sang about the changing colours, storm-grey billows and swirling flecks of white. And as he sang, the waters rose and spread out as far as he could see. And above, the emptiness filled with moving air, clouds blew on the wind, and rain fell into the waters below.

He sang of the great lights that light up the sky. Lightning flashed for a moment, wild and bright. Everything that there was was split in two, and then it was gone. Skyrunner sang on. He sang of the myriad stars that light up the night sky. And he sang of the greater lights, the moon and the sun, who run such great distances across the sky by night and by day.

He sang of the seashore, and as he danced along the seashore at dawn, the land was separated from the sea. He sang of the plains and the mountains. And he leapt from felltop to felltop, and he sang of the deep valleys that spread out from the mountains in the middle. He sang of the lakes and the rivers. And for all of the fells and the plains and the lakes and the rivers he sang their shapes, their faces, their names.

I will not spend a long time telling you about these things. These are the more-or-less permanent fixtures of the world. And though many things have changed since then, the land and the sea and the sky remain the same. And the greater and lesser lights still do what they have always done, and the seas rise and fall as they always have done.

And Skyrunner sang about other things, living things. The trees, oak and ash and birch and elm, and blackthorn, hawthorn, whin, and briar and bramble. And there were other trees that filled the forests, and shrubs that covered the moorlands. And there were birds too, wakening from their eggs, pecking into the sunlight.

But all these things you will know as well. I will not tell you everything he sang. Skyrunner sang all these things, and they were there.

Many musicians play their instruments well, fiddles and harps and flutes. But Skyrunner's instrument was his voice. His voice and his songs. With those songs, he could conjure scenes and landscapes. With his voice, he could create sense and feeling. His voice was precious and all his own. But the songs themselves were songs that Skyrunner had heard before. He had learned them long ago from other singers. Those were ancient songs that Skyrunner sang now for his new listeners.

* * *

And it was finished.

And the world was so very different from when he had begun. The sea, the land, the sky, mountains and forests, valleys and lakes and streams, and the sound of the wind, and the music of waterfalls, and the sweetness of birdsong. And Skyrunner walked in the world, and he visited many places. Everywhere was beautiful, and it was just as he had imagined it would be. And as he moved through the world he started to look for a place where he could make his home.

The people he met were all pleasant enough, but a place to stay was hard to find.

"You should have better luck in the next valley. I completely understand your situation. I had a long search before I found this place. I'm sure you can see it is a great place for me. I'm sure you will find a great place soon."

"Yes, I quite understand. I found this position with no trouble at all. But I have heard that some people have to search for a long time before they find a place. I heard once about someone who had to search for months before he found a good place in Yewdale. I don't think I could be pleased to live in Yewdale after having lived here. No, I don't think I would want to move to Yewdale. But he seems happy with it. I'm sure you will find somewhere soon that you will be happy with."

"Yes, I have heard it's difficult now, to find somewhere. Many people are looking, I have heard. But if you carry on I'm sure you will find somewhere."

"Oh, I didn't realise you were wanting to stay here. No, that wouldn't really work. But I'm sure you will find somewhere of your own soon. Did you try in the next valley? You should have better luck there."

"For someone of your talent I would have thought it would be easy to find somewhere to stay. I didn't mean here, of course. Somewhere else."

"I would have thought you would have found somewhere to stay by now."

And sometimes when they met up, those people in their high halls, they would share the news of what they had seen or what they had heard. Sometimes they would have news about Skyrunner. About who he had visited, or where he had been seen. But then the news about Skyrunner seemed to stop. No-one was quite sure when it happened. At first they thought he had simply found somewhere to stay. But no-one seemed to know where it was. So it seemed Skyrunner had disappeared. And before too long no-one spoke about Skyrunner any more.

The Tree of Knowledge

This is a story about something that happened long ago, in the days when the Elders first came to Highgarth.

It was late one midwinter's night, and a stranger came knocking at the gate.

"Will you give me lodging for the night?" he said.

Outside, it was cold, it was quiet, and above all, everything was dark. So the Elders brought a lamp to see who it was who was knocking. The man at the gate was dressed in a cloak made of many different fragments of rags, all sewn together. His staff was like the branch of a living tree, with green leaves sprouting at intervals along its length. His head was covered, but he flung back the hood of his cloak to reveal his shocking red hair. The Elders knew that it was unlucky to turn away a stranger who came to call late at night, so he was invited in.

* * *

The stranger was grateful for the shelter he had been given, and the next morning he was on his way.

"I will reward you for your kindness," the stranger said. "I don't have much to offer you, and I see that you are surrounded by riches in this place. But I will leave you my staff."

He plunged his staff into the ground in the middle of the courtyard there.

"This staff will grow into a tree. You may think it looks like a hazel tree, but this will be unlike any other hazel tree you know.

It will grow faster than you think, and it will flower and bear nuts. When the nuts are on the tree, any one of you who breaks the shell and eats the nut will gain all the knowledge that there is in the world, good and bad. That is what I give to you."

And with that, the stranger covered his red hair with the hood of his cloak, and he walked away.

* * *

The Elders hardly knew what to think about the staff that stood there, stuck into the ground in the middle of the yard. But they left it where it was, and soon enough, it became clear that it was no ordinary staff. Just as the stranger had said, the staff took root, and it grew quickly, tall and strong, and soon there was a full-grown hazel tree standing in the yard.

When the snow melted and spring came, catkins appeared on the tree, and by the end of the summer, clusters of nuts were hanging there.

Mindrace saw all this, and he was keen to eat a nut from the tree and gain the knowledge that the stranger had promised.

But Blossom said: "How can we trust that stranger's words? He promised many great things, but what if he was trying to trick us? If Mindrace eats the fruit and he is killed by poison, this would be bad for us. Someone should taste and try the nuts from this strange tree, before we risk our leader."

In those days, there was one there with the Elders who was called Mind. Mind said: "I can be the one to test the nuts. I can take the risk, and I am prepared to protect our leader."

As soon as he ate the nut, Mind was overwhelmed. Suddenly he saw everything clearly. He saw why things were the way they were, or what had been done in the past to make things the way they were, or to make things happen the way they had. He saw how the decisions the Elders were making could only lead to loss, disgrace, and despair. And he saw that he would not be able to persuade them to do things any other way. He saw beautiful visions, and he knew with certainty that they were impossible dreams.

Mind found it hard to concentrate on any one thing. He was an expert in so many different areas, he was easily distracted, and his thoughts couldn't help but start to look at things from other viewpoints, and continue to wander, chasing unexpected aspects that uncovered and revealed themselves. Very quickly he became depressed. He saw that there was no good way out of the situation he found himself in. He only saw the end.

The next morning, the Elders found him. He had hung himself from a low branch of that hazel tree.

"Now there is a new nut hanging from the tree," Mindrace said. "Cut him down."

* * *

When they saw what had happened to Mind, the Elders started to argue about what they should do next.

"He ate, and he died," Blossom said. "The nut was deadly. He sacrificed himself for all our sakes."

"Those nuts are not poisonous," Heave said. "A weak-minded man was not well-suited to this job."

"Whether it was a conventional poison or not, it killed him," Herder said. "I call that poison."

"I should eat a nut from the tree," Mindrace said. "True power only comes with great knowledge."

"Knowledge leads to despair, as we have seen," Fairhair said. "Be careful!"

The Elders continued to discuss this, and they failed to reach a consensus about what they thought Mindrace should do. But Mindrace himself was determined that he would eat the nut from the tree. And so that is what happened.

* * *

Small birds chattered on a branch as Mindrace stood beneath the tree, and he listened to what they were saying.

One said: "Here comes Mindrace. He thinks he will gain knowledge of all the world, but that knowledge is gone. That knowledge all went to one man, and that man died with it."

Another said: "For years he will wander though the world, seeking knowledge. He had a chance to find it here, but that chance is gone."

A third said: "Nuts are ripe and good to eat."

A fourth said: "Giants who walk by day I fear more than those who walk by night."

A fifth said: "Those who fail to take a chance may regret it for a long time."

A sixth said: "A missed chance may not come again."

"Nuts are ripe and good to eat," said the third.

"Here comes Mindrace," said the first.

And Mindrace knew that the chance was gone, and that the nuts would be worthless to him. But he picked a nut from the hazel tree. He cracked the shell under a stone. He bit into the sweet kernel. It tasted good. And that was all.

The Pursuit of Mindrace

Rush dreamed a dream one night as he lay in bed. The dream worried him very much, so he went the next morning to ask his mother whether she could understand what it meant.

"I dreamed I saw an old man in a grey coat. He had a long grey beard and grey skin. I dreamed I was standing with him in some faraway place. I thought it was a mountaintop, but I looked again and I saw that we were in a forest, and I looked again and it was as though we were underwater. That old man was speaking to me all the time. It sounded like wonderful speech, but although I wanted to, I couldn't understand a word. Tell me, mother, what can it mean?"

"The old man is easy to recognise," she said. "He is Mindrace. He knows a great many things. There are few who know more. He is always searching for new knowledge. He will wander far and wide to get it, and he is never satisfied. When you saw him talking to you, it means that if you find him you will become wise. And when you didn't understand, it means that you are still young, and there are many things that you do not know. But if you go out into the world and try to find him, perhaps you will learn something."

"Yes," Rush answered. "I will go at once."

"Before you go, I will give you some advice," said his mother.

But Rush said: "I don't need any more advice. Soon I will find that old man, and he will tell me everything I need to know."

So Rush put on his walking clothes, and he set out across the wild heathland. His mother stood at the gate and watched him go, but Rush did not look back.

Out in the wilderness there was no-one around. Rush could hear the birds chattering high in the sky, but they were too high for him to see. Sometimes birds flew out from the heather in front of him. And sometimes he saw some of the golden sheep that roam over those moors. He walked for many days, but he saw no sign of the old man in the grey coat.

It was the fifteenth day. The time drew on to evening, and day turned into dusk. Rush caught sight of a long house that was standing in a small cluster of trees underneath the fellside. He headed for the house and he knocked on the door.

An old man answered, and Rush said: "I have come to ask for shelter for the night. I have been walking for fifteen days."

The man invited Rush into the house. Although it was growing dark outside, the inside of the house was not as gloomy as Rush would have expected. There were lamps of a kind that he had not seen before, and there were many things there made of polished metal, hanging on the walls and standing on tables and on the floor, so the inside of the house seemed to sparkle.

"You must be hungry after such a long time walking," said the man. "Come and sit down."

The man brought out dishes of fine food: roast beef, turnips, and cabbage, and there was ale too, in glasses inlaid with shining colours.

"This is very good food," said Rush. "I didn't expect to see so many riches in a house with one old man so far away from anywhere. Tell me who you are."

This is what the man said: "Well for the first, we are not so far away from everywhere. There are many places close to here. Many of them are fine and special places, though perhaps few people know about them.

"But if you are wondering how I manage to be so rich. That is easy to explain. I own a flock of sheep, and their fleeces are made of pure gold. Those sheep are hardy enough that they need little looking after, and they roam out on the fell. But once a year, I round up the sheep and bring them in for shearing.

"Some of the gold I have fashioned into wonderful objects. You can see some of them in this room. Some of the gold I use to buy the finest food and drink, such as you have eaten tonight. And more is filling the mattresses of the many beds in the house, or is hidden under the floor or in the roof, because I cannot spend it all."

"My name is Herder," said the man. "I don't suppose you knew this before or you would not have asked."

"Now I will offer you something," the man went on. "Stay here with me. The truth is, I am old now. I can hardly cope, running this place on my own, and I think I will soon die. I have no children to take over this flock. Stay here and help me while I am alive, and all this will soon be yours."

Then the old man showed Rush where he could sleep that night.

In the morning, Herder said: "Have you decided whether you will stay here with me?"

Rush said: "When I left my home, I came away with one thing in mind. My aim is to find Mindrace. I don't know whether you have heard of him. It may be that news from the wide world rarely reaches such a distant spot as this. But I can tell you this: Mindrace is the wisest man that I have heard tell of. And if I find him, he will teach me everything that I could wish to know."

Herder said: "You may be surprised to hear it, but Mindrace was here only a few days ago."

"I am glad to hear this," said Rush. "Can you tell me which way he went?"

"Will you not stay here?" asked Herder. "I can tell you that Mindrace was not happy when I saw him pass by here. It might not be good to meet him."

"No, I must find Mindrace," said Rush.

And the old man pointed away towards the fells. "That way," he said, "you will find Mindrace."

Rush walked out in the direction that Herder had said, and he didn't look back. It was a steep climb at first, but before too long, he was on a grassy ridge, and he could walk on easily while the land fell away steeply to his right and left. He followed that ridge as far as it went, then he had to drop down before climbing up again. This went on for several days, but in all that time, Rush never saw any sign of an old man in a grey coat. The only signs of life he saw were the birds that flew high above him, calling and chattering in the sky.

As Rush walked on, the high landscapes grew rougher and rockier, and more and more covered in heather. Several days had passed. The sun sank behind the ridges, and day turned into dusk, and Rush descended into a valley where birch trees were growing by the shore of a large lake. He saw a small group of wooden buildings in the trees, and he headed for those buildings.

Rush knocked on the door, and a girl answered.

Rush said: "I have come to ask for shelter for the night. I have been walking for longer than I can remember."

The girl said: "Come in. I will have to ask my father about this, but I am certain that he will be very glad that you have come." Then the girl disappeared, and before long a man came in.

"My name is Buttertub," said the man. "You must be hungry. Sit down, and my daughter Girth will bring you something to eat."

So Rush sat down at the table. The room was rustic and homely. The oak benches and the table were solid and plain, and the plaster walls were painted with scenes and blooming floral patterns. When Girth brought in a bowl of curds, she brushed his hand with her hand. And when she brought a large lump of butter for him to eat with his bread, she trod on his foot with her foot.

"Now I have something to say to you," Buttertub said. "Stay here with us on the farm. The truth is, I have been hoping a good young man would pass by here, for my daughter's sake. There are only two of us on the farm. It is a pleasant enough place, and we do well enough, but often I worry that my daughter gets lonely here with only her father for company. It's clear the two of you are a good match. Stay here and marry my daughter."

After supper, Rush and Girth sat on the lakeshore. The moon was reflected clear in the water like a great round cheese. Now she was a lot less shy, and she had both her arms around him.

This is what Rush said to her: "You may be interested to hear about why I came out walking in the world. I am looking for Mindrace. He is the wisest of all men. When I find him, he will teach me everything I could wish to know."

The next morning, the high pikes overlooking the lake were glowing red as the sun rose.

Buttertub said: "Will you not stay here? I can see that you are a fine young man, and my daughter Girth will be disappointed to see you go."

Rush said: "I am looking for Mindrace. I mean to find him, and then he will tell me all manner of things, and I will become very wise. Did you see him come this way?"

Buttertub said: "I did see an old man in a grey coat. He was here only a few days ago. But I would not chase after him if I were you. He looked furious, and if you spend much longer wandering in the wilderness chasing that man, it could drive you mad."

"Tell me, which way did he go?" Rush said.

"That way," Buttertub said, "you will find Mindrace," and he pointed away up the hill.

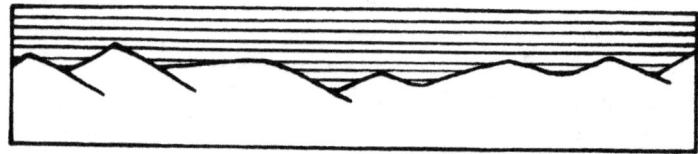

Rush climbed up into the mountains again, the way that Buttertub had told him. Sometimes he walked and sometimes he ran. The land was high and the ground was rough. Whenever he thought he had found a path, it soon grew vague and indistinct. He was high on the fells, and he could see a long way. But no matter how hard he looked into the distance, he could see no sign of the old man in the grey coat. Sometimes he saw something moving, but it was always only a bird or a fox or one of the golden sheep that live up on those fells. Often he thought that he must have walked over that same stretch of moorland already. Everything looked familiar. Everything looked the same.

But after several days, the weather grew worse. Clouds circled the highest peaks, and mist rolled down from there until it filled the valleys. Rush carried on walking as long as he could, but after a while he could see no further than a few yards.

"I will have to go down," he thought to himself. "I don't know which way I am walking up here."

He thought he could see which way was downhill, and he started to make his way slowly in that direction.

As he descended through the mist, the slope grew steeper. Wet rocks slipped and slid beneath his feet. Small stones went bouncing and rattling out of sight into the mist, falling towards the depths of the valley below.

Rush stepped onto a slab of rock, and it began to slide beneath his feet. He quickly leapt off the slab, but it continued to slide downhill. He stood still on the stony slope as the boulder slid out of sight, down into the pale grey depths.

Rush could see nothing of what happened next. He could only hear the sounds that emerged through the blind whiteness. The sigh and clatter of rushing and sliding rocks did not die down, but rather grew to a roar like thunder. There came a sharp crack that Rush guessed could only be the sound of mighty boulders splitting against one another, but the roar did not stop. It seemed to grow even more, though it now seemed more distant. Some of the sounds he could hear must have been echoes from unseen mountains all around him.

At last the rumbling stopped, and all was silent again.

Rush could still see little in any direction. He reckoned his best option was just to carry on down in the direction he had been going. He took the descent very carefully, and it was a long time before he emerged from the mist. Then he saw the huge pile of rocks that had fallen down the fell. It seemed that the rockfall had narrowly missed a small house, and Rush made his way over to it.

As he approached the house, a small man leapt out of the door, and ran towards him. The man started speaking when he was still some distance away from Rush: "I saw you coming down the fell," he said. "Was it you that pushed all these rocks off the mountain?"

"I did it," said Rush, "but I didn't mean to do it."

"You have done us a great service," said the man. "There has been a troll here who has been causing us great distress. He would often eat the livestock of the farmers who live in this valley, and sometimes he would even go into the village and take one of the ladies or maidens to eat. And you have killed that troll.

"The troll was sitting here, eating my sheep. When the rocks came thundering down from the mountain, he didn't even move. A huge boulder struck his skull and split it into many pieces. He was killed at once. You must come with me to the village, and we will let them know the good news."

The village in that valley was surrounded by fence of wooden staves, and smoke rose from the chimneys of the houses up into the mist.

"This fence was little use against the troll", said the shepherd. "He could easily step over it or kick it down with his toe."

As they approached the village, another man came out running towards them. He started shouting: "What has happened? We all heard a great rumble, like thunder."

"That was no thunder," said the shepherd. "This young man pushed a lot of rocks off the mountain. They hit the troll, and they killed it dead."

"Is the troll dead?" said the man from the village.

"Yes, I saw it myself," said the shepherd.

"And," the man from the village turned to Rush, "you pushed the rocks?"

"I did it," said Rush.

"Now that you have killed the troll that was haunting our village, you must become our leader," said the man.

"I don't know about that," Rush said. "If I killed the troll, it was an accident."

"Modesty will only get you so far," said the man from the village. "The truth is, we are all impressed with you, and our village needs a leader. Ridding us of the troll in the way that you did was surely a great deed. Stay here and lead us. We are all in agreement."

That night, a feast was held in the village to celebrate the deliverance from the troll, and of course Rush sat in the highest seat at the table.

The next morning, the man from the village said to Rush: "Have you decided whether you will stay here to lead us?"

Rush said: "I have been walking for a long time with one thing in mind. My aim is to find Mindrace, as he is the wisest man that I have heard tell of. When I find him, he will tell me all manner of things, and I will become very wise. So tell me, did you see him come this way?"

The man from the village said: "I can tell you this: There was an old man with a long beard who left here only yesterday."

"I am glad to hear it," said Rush. "Can you tell me which way he went?"

"Will you not stay here?" asked the man from the village. "I would not try to find that old man if I were you. He was not happy when he left here, and it could be hard for you to catch him."

"Tell me which way he went," said Rush.

And the man from the village pointed up into the mountains. "That way," he said, "you will find Mindrace."

Rush walked away in the direction the man had said. He reached a stream, and he followed that stream up through a narrow valley that was filled with oak trees. The ground was covered in rocks, and the rocks were slippery and damp with spray from the tumbling beck. After a little while, he reached a place where the trees suddenly ended, the valley widened, and the stream slowed. As he looked out beyond the edge of the trees, Rush found that he had climbed so high that he was inside a cloud. An area of dead flat land stretched out in front of him, though in the mist he could not see how far it reached. And he sensed that there were high slopes that encircled the flat area, but he couldn't see them clearly.

Through the mist in front of him, he heard a voice calling to him: "What are you looking for?"

"I am looking for Mindrace," called Rush into the mist. "If I find him, I believe he will teach me everything I could wish to know."

The voice came again: "And did you not find anything on your way here that could satisfy you?"

"Why would I stop in any of those places, or how could I be satisfied?" Rush replied. "I came to find Mindrace, and I didn't find him in any of the places I passed by."

Then the voice said: "And did you learn anything on your way here?"

"I know this," Rush replied. "Mindrace is the wisest man that I have heard tell of, and when I find him, he will teach me all I need to know, and then I will be wise."

"I am Mindrace," said the voice. "Come over to me, then, and perhaps after all this time you will learn something."

So Rush walked out into the quiet flat area in front of him. The mist meant that he soon lost any sense of what surrounded him. Underfoot it grew wetter and wetter. He strained to see whether he could catch a glimpse of the old man in front of him. For a while, all he saw was pale grey. But then all at once in all the grey nothingness, Rush thought perhaps he could make out a form. A grey figure, standing some way ahead of him. He leapt forward, but as he did so the ground beneath his feet gave way, and he found himself sinking in the mire. He couldn't go forward, and he couldn't go back. Soon he was in over his head.

On the far side of the marsh, Mindrace stood and watched. His grey coat shimmered. His grey beard was full of the mist. He stood steady with his staff planted on firm ground. And when he was satisfied that everything was quiet and still in the marsh, he turned and walked away.

The Rose-Tinted Dwarf

"I know of a dwarf who lives on the moors. It is a desolate spot. There is little to recommend it. That dwarf has grown so old, his beard hangs down to his ankles and trails in the dirt, yet still he does not cut it. His clothes are worn and tattered. That dwarf is too lazy to look after himself. He looks miserable to be living alone in that place, and yet still he stays."

The dwarf says: "Though it is not much to look at now, I will not abandon this place, always dear to me, left in ruins by the shameful deeds of others.

"I remember the glorious days of the past. I was a gardener, and this was my garden. Many things have changed since then.

"In those days I was famous, not for being a bitter miser, but for the beautiful garden I had made. Many came here to see that garden. It was a great wonder. Many things have changed since then, and more will change soon.

"In the days before the Elders came, many were the flowers that bloomed here. And my sweet-scented roses I loved and prized above all the others. The garden stretched further than your eyes can see, and the summer evenings were pink and orange. Many things have changed since then, and more will change soon.

"I don't know where they came from, and I don't know why they came. It is difficult for me to fathom. Who would come to a place filled with beauty and destroy it, lay it low, make it worthless?

"Now when I look out over the place where the flowers once grew, I see only desolate moorlands. But I stay here so that I can more easily remember what I once had. I peer back in time at what was lost, though it seems it will not return while I am alive. But some summer evenings the sky glows bright and vivid with the colours of the roses that once grew in this place. Then I feel a little closer. I feel a glimmer of the forgotten glory. And then the sun sets."

"Tell me then, if you know so much: Who was it who destroyed that garden, or who was the dwarf who made it?"

"The dwarf calls himself Roseglad, though others may call him Rosetint, and his memory of what happened there is not the same as mine.

"It is true that he had a large hoard there on the moorland, of a certain rock. It is true that that rock was fair to look at, rosy blushing, sparkling pink and orange. We were sent by Smith to fetch the rock. Only Smith knew what was hidden in it, only he knew how he could use it to make some of the great treasures that form the foundations of our world. And it is true that we came and took it. That much is true.

"But that dwarf was happy enough to see all his red rock leaving with us. The truth is, we did a deal with the dwarf. He was happy enough to do it. Who knows how long he sat there, smug on the moorland, rich in gold, once those rocks had gone. Now he tells his story to anyone who will listen, but he was eager enough to give us those rocks for a good price. It seems he regrets it now."

The dwarf says: "I hardly wonder what value Smith found in those worthless red rocks. That matter is hardly worth my consideration. More I worry about the flowers trampled by the bumbling oafs as they traipsed through the garden. All was ruined, kicked down, uprooted. Everything was well here before they came, and those roses will never grow again."

Bright Shining Sun

Beyond the horizon, there is a bright house, well built, with a high roof. It stands there alone, and every morning a young man leaves that house to go out running. That man's name is Shiner.

It was early when Shiner's mother said: "It would be better for you not to go outside. The weather is bad today. There is only unpleasantness out there. Better to stay here, both safe and warm."

Shiner said: "The weather is no better or worse than any other day, the weather may be different, but that is hardly a reason to stay here and do nothing. How many times have you been out in what you call bad weather? I would far rather be out in the weather than waiting at home, watching it pass me by."

Shiner's mother said: "There are many dangers outside. You think you know so much, but there is a great deal that you do not yet know, and more that you never will. There are many dangers that you will not see until it is too late."

Shiner said: "Many times I have run the way I will run today. I know well what I may meet out there. When did you run there last? There is more to lose by staying at home, letting time disappear."

Shiner's mother said: "Stay at home today. The world is wide, the sky is high, it will be hard for you to run these great distances. I can see your pain. Your body will not stand it. You will probably also get lost in the vastness of the world. It would be better to stay here and rest. Wait for better times that will surely come soon."

Shiner said: "What do you want, mother? That I should stay at home with you and grow old, out of sight of the world? That I should waste my best days resting here? Soon I will be old, and I don't want to look back and remember how I waited for a moment to arrive. I have often heard your voice urging me to rest and do nothing."

Shiner's mother said: "I have often seen you run before you are ready, and often seen you return disheartened, limping, and hurt."

Shiner said: "I have seen a girl out there, mother. She is fast. I have not seen anyone run as fast. Do you suppose I will catch that girl if I sit here with you, waiting idly as time passes?"

Shiner's mother said: "Listen to me. If you want to run quickly enough to catch any girl, you should let your body recover. Rest now, and start slowly."

Shiner said: "I am young and I am strong. Perhaps you have forgotten the feeling of a strong and powerful body. No doubt I am stronger now than you ever were. It is difficult for you to understand how I am feeling."

Shiner's mother said: "I see that you are determined to go, and that nothing I can say will persuade you otherwise. But if you go out today, will you not take a horse? I will give you a fine horse, pale gold in colour, with a shining mane. This horse is fast, I don't know of a faster horse, and he can run easily and quickly through the sky. The horse is called Lightfoot, and I would be glad to give him to you. Then you could rest your legs. I am sure this endless running will take a toll on your body, no matter how strong you feel now."

Shiner said: "And what would people say, mother, if they saw me riding a horse? Is he so weak that he cannot run himself? Has he begun to grow old and infirm? What would that girl say when she saw me approach her on horseback? Is he too slow to catch me on his own two legs? Does he have to rely on a beast to do his running for him?"

Shiner's mother said: "If this is what you are thinking, you may not know this: few people actually look at you as you approach. You may think that men are pleased to see you, but you may not know that they turn their eyes away as you come near. They do not dare to look too closely at you. They do not dare to stare at the bright glory of your body. The truth is: few people would know that you rode on horseback rather than running. No-one could stand to look long enough to see."

Shiner said: "Mother, you underestimate my own strength and speed. This horse Lightfoot may run quickly, but I suppose I can run faster myself. I am not sure the horse is up to the task. How would I feel, sitting in the saddle while that horse ambles steadily across the sky? If I should meet anyone, I would be ashamed. I can hardly believe they would not notice that I was riding and not running as I have always done before. And whether they see it or not, I would know it. I would feel it. Is that what you want? If by some chance I was to catch that girl today, would you want me to feel shame and disgrace?"

Shiner's mother said: "I see you are determined to ignore my advice and go out running, though you are hurt, and I can hardly believe you will run far without making things worse for yourself. But before you go, I will give you a drink to give you strength and ease your pain. I have mixed this wine with certain herbs that grow only here on the Shimmering Plain. Drink it."

"Thank-you, mother," Shiner said. And he drank the drink that was in the cup that his mother handed to him.

Before long, Shiner was ready to leave. And so the gates opened, and he went out. He started to run, first across the moor that surrounds that desolate place, and then stepping up into the sky. Faster he ran, and even faster, climbing higher and higher.

His legs and his body glowed, and the faster he went, the brighter he shone.

There was no uneven ground that could cause him to misstep. He would not lose his footing, or fall and twist an ankle or a knee as many do who try to run quickly over rough terrain. Inside he burned with fury.

And as he ran, Shiner was thinking about the muscles in his legs. He wanted to run within his limits. Because in truth, he was all too aware of his past injuries. Aware of things in his body that had not quite recovered. At that moment he felt fine, but how would it be if he ran a little faster? Or how would he feel after he had been running hard all day long? How would he feel then? Shiner ran on.

High in the sky, everything was empty. He ran for hours, on and further on, but there was no sign of the girl today. And even though he peered into the distance, Shiner could not see her.

"And I could hardly run after her if I did see her today. How could I catch her when my legs are hurt? How can I run as fast as her when I am limping and in pain? And If I did catch her, how could I speak to her in this mood? What would I say? I am overwhelmed by pain. I feel I should stop running now. And if I stopped, I am sure I would barely be able to walk. And my legs will not be better tomorrow.

"It is good that I cannot see her. It is good that I will never catch her when I am not at my best. I can only hope she doesn't appear now over some horizon, and decide that today is the day that she will chase me. What would I say to her then?"

And Shiner took all the speed out of his legs, and he slowed to a walk. He would have to walk the last few miles home. The pain didn't stop. This was not the burning exhilaration of muscles well used. This would not be better in the morning. Something was wrong, again. Something was torn, swollen, inflamed.

The gates were open as Shiner limped home. And his mother was standing outside to welcome him back.

The Duck Thief

There was a man who lived by the seashore. That man was called Shoreguard, and the farm where he lived was called Grange. In those days, the landscape at Grange was rather different from how it is now. When the tide came in, the sea would race across the sands almost all the way to the farmhouse. It is hard to imagine it, as nowadays Grange is a long way from the sea.

Shoreguard was a duck farmer, and he kept his ducks on a long lagoon that was separated from the sea by a long, low, muddy bank. Shoreguard was so old that he could barely walk. But every day he would go down to the lagoon to feed the ducks. When the ducks saw him coming, they would all fly over, flapping and splashing, as quickly as they could. And every month, when Shoreguard walked, very slowly, the long mile to the market, leaning heavily on his sturdy staff, and wrapped up in a heavy cloak against the weather, the ducks followed after him in a long line.

Although Shoreguard was a simple duck farmer, he dressed very well, in silk and fine furs. And the house at Grange was richly decorated with wonderful carved objects and gilded ornaments. The people who used to visit Shoreguard to buy duck eggs were all amazed by the expensive craftsmanship that was on show around the farm. And rumours spread in that district about Shoreguard and his wealth. Many people who came to visit Shoreguard at Grange said that they wanted to buy eggs, but really they just wanted a chance to see the curious old man with his fancy-looking farm.

Some people said that Shoreguard was a former warrior, and that there were chests of gold won in war hidden underneath his house. Others said that Shoreguard was a powerful magician with otherworldly contacts. Some even said that he was an elf himself.

* * *

There was a man who lived in that district. Everyone called him Goldeneye because he often gazed longingly at anything that was made of gold. Unfortunately for Goldeneye, many of the things he wanted were out of his reach.

Late one evening a man came knocking at the door of the farmhouse where Goldeneye lived with his wife. It was a small man with shocking red hair.

"Are you a dwarf or an elf," Goldeneye asked him. "Or why have you come here?"

"My name is Robin," said the red-haired man. "I was out walking, and I stopped here to ask for shelter for the night."

"Come in," said Goldeneye. "You must be hungry. Sit down, and my wife will bring us all food to eat."

So the two of them sat at the table, and Goldeneye's wife served up the best food: mashed turnips and oatmeal and butter, and there was beer to drink. And so they all ate very well.

When they had finished eating, Robin and Goldeneye were still sitting at the table, and Robin said: "Can you believe how rich Shoreguard is? He sits all day by that pool with no-one there but all those ducks. How does he live such a lifestyle? It seems to me that he has some sort of secret. And if anyone should discover the source of his riches, it would not be hard to take that away from him."

Goldeneye said: "I know how to find this out. Not far from here there is a bird they call Widefaring. They say that bird knows many things. I am sure that bird will know all about Shoreguard."

Robin said: "You are right. It might be an idea to ask that bird."

No more was said on that subject that evening, and after a little while, they were all asleep.

* * *

When Goldeneye awoke the next morning, the red-haired man had disappeared. But Goldeneye didn't wait long to act on what he had heard the night before. He left his house at once and walked down to the seashore, and before long he had found the pole where the seagull usually sat.

Goldeneye said: "I have come to ask you about the duck farmer, Shoreguard."

Widefaring said: "It is good that you have come to me to ask about this. I am known for flying far and wide to gather knowledge from all the world. But I am not ignorant of what happens here close to home, almost within sight of this very pole where I sit."

Goldeneye said: "Tell me then about Shoreguard and his wealth."

Widefaring said: "I have heard about other birds who rely on their sight alone, barely moving from their perch, lazy in their wings, overconfident in their eyes. I am sure those birds cannot even see me now as I sit here on this pole. After all, where are they? I cannot see them. Those birds could hardly fathom the strange things that happen at Shoreguard's farm. After all, I have been to that farm and that pond myself. I have seen it all, and yet still I can barely fathom it."

Goldeneye said: "Tell me then, how does Shoreguard get his wealth, or how may I take it for myself?"

Widefaring said: "You are right to ask me. I know well the answers to your questions. Others may talk more than me but say less.

"I have eaten many of the wisest fish in that pond. I cannot understand how their great knowledge passes from my belly into my memory. This is one of the three great mysteries. But this is not something I need to understand. I eat the fish, and my mind grows. I remember all that those fish ever saw. How many fish has Farseer eaten? I know this for a fact: few fish fly to the top of the fell where he sits motionless every day.

"The second mystery is this: I have flown many times around the whole world, and yet every time I fly, I find new places. How can this be? Does the world change so much? I have seen so many things, and I remember even more. Few know more than I do.

"The third mystery is this: Every day I see new things, and I remember even more. I find that my mind has grown. How can this be? Though my knowledge may seem unsurpassed, every day I find that I know more than I knew the day before.

"There is a tree in my mind that grows quickly. It sprouts new branches and green leaves. The tree trunk grows thicker and stronger with each passing day. Long ago I thought of a great tree in my mind, but since then the tree has grown so much. When I look back at what I saw then, what I thought of as a great tree, I see that it was no more than a stripling bush, short and fragile. How can this be?

"I know of another mystery: A bird who sits still on a mountain-top and refuses to fly anywhere still claims to see what happens in the whole world. How can this be? This is surely the greatest mystery of all."

Goldeneye said: "I would like it very much if you could tell me about Shoreguard and his wealth."

Widefaring said: "That is easy for me to tell you. There is no mystery there.

"Shoreguard has many ducks. All of them look quite alike, and I cannot tell them apart. And yet still one of the ducks is different from the others. That duck is called Goldander, and the eggs it lays are made of pure gold.

When Goldeneye had heard what he came there to hear, he went away from that place.

* * *

The next day, Goldeneye was feeling particularly pleased with himself. He could hardly have hoped things could have gone so well. He was sitting outside the house enjoying the taste of a drink of beer and the smell of the food his wife was cooking. The weather was pleasant and mild. The future seemed suddenly full of promise. It was as though everything had taken a turn for the better since the red-haired man had come to call.

When the food was ready, Goldeneye and his wife sat down to eat. And Goldeneye said:

"I have a feeling we will soon be rather richer than we have been until now. You will have new clothes, all in scarlet cloth and embroidered with gold thread. We will buy cattle, and eat from golden plates. And I would very much like a sword made from the purest gold. That would suit me well.

"And how will this happen?" she said.

"You should not worry about that," he said.

"I have done some good business. You may see certain changes taking place. But it is best if you leave these things to me."

"Husband," she said. "I am lucky that I married you. You know so much, and I am very much looking forward to all these things that you will bring to me."

"Tell me, wife, what is this delicious stew that you have cooked for us this evening that we have been eating?"

"You, husband, were kind and thoughtful enough to bring home a fat duck yesterday. So I cooked this duck in the stew for you to eat."

It was difficult for Goldeneye to take in this news. Perhaps that is why he appeared so calm, he had not fully understood what had happened. Perhaps he was still so overcome by the sense of great satisfaction that he had been feeling all that day that he could not fully appreciate the great loss that had befallen him. Perhaps he was still pleased with himself after his unexpected success in the theft of the duck. Perhaps he was satisfied from the fine duck stew that his wife had prepared with such care and skill, anxious to show her appreciation for the man who promised so much. Perhaps the calm had been brought on by the fine weather. Or perhaps he was drunk, and couldn't understand what was happening. But there was no angry outburst, and there was no sudden change in Goldeneye. But he never really recovered after that.

* * *

"All this happened a long time ago!" said the hawk to the red-haired boy on the mountaintop.

"Nowadays, the sea does not come close to the place where the old farm stood at Grange, even at high tide, and most of the lagoon has been drained. But there is a small pond there, where the ducks still live."

And the red-haired boy pulled his cloak around him as the wind blew. He looked out to the south in the direction the bird had said. The mountains fell away, and a long lake stretched away, bright silver among the blue-grey hills below. And further in the far distance, there might have been the sea. But over where the bird had told him about the farm and the pond and the place where the sea used to be, everything seemed pale blue and paler grey, and the clouds moved overhead, blown by the wind that gusted in his face. His eyes were watery with the wind, and he couldn't be sure he could see.

The Winning of Fairway of Highlife

There was once a farmer's son of little consequence. He was called Langdale after the place where he was born. The boy's father was also called Langdale, so sometimes people would call the son young Langdale to tell the two of them apart.

One time, young Langdale was playing out in the field with some other boys from that district. They had a ball, and they were throwing the ball to each other. While this was going on, a woman came walking. She was very tall, and very beautiful. She looked a lot like a giantess.

Langdale had the ball in his hands. He had never seen anything like this woman before. No woman he had ever seen had been as tall or as beautiful. The dress she wore was plain and light and long, her hair was dark, and was tied back, and her face seemed free of cares. Langdale called out to the woman, but she simply strode on as though she had not heard him. Langdale felt an urge inside him. He had to get the woman's attention. So he threw the ball over to where she was walking.

The woman stopped. Her expression changed in an instant. She fixed Langdale with a stare that could cause running water to freeze or cause the wind to change.

"You shouldn't throw your ball at me," she said. "Now I will curse you: you will find no rest here in this valley, Langdale. You will find no peace here. You will never be satisfied until you have found a girl called Fairway who lives far away from here, across the sea."

Then the woman turned and went on her way. Langdale knew well that the way the woman was walking was a dead end, and the only way she would be able to get out of the valley would be to climb up into the highest fells.

The other boys fled, and Langdale was left alone at the bottom of the valley, thinking of nothing but the strange woman and the words of her curse. He had to go and fetch his ball back himself.

Langdale did not think about leaving at once. He stayed in the valley at his father's house for some time. Every day, the sun rose over the eastern ridge and set behind the western ridge. The valley bottom saw the sunlight for some hours, but whether the sun was shining or not, very little happened there. The steep fellsides that surrounded the valley rose up like impassable high walls, covered in bracken, and broken by tall grey cliffs. They cast long shadows, and Langdale felt hemmed in. He often wondered about the curse and the girl, and where she might be, and one day he went to ask his father's advice.

"I don't know much about that," the elder Langdale said. "I don't know much about giantesses or curses, or where you might find magic girls. You should go to the summer fair at Marradale. You will find someone there, I bet."

So when the time came, Langdale went to Marradale for the summer fair. There was music and dancing and beer to drink, and the sun shone late into the evening. And everywhere there were girls and young men showing off to whoever they thought they might catch. But Langdale was not satisfied. Something was missing. And when he came back home, he was more restless than ever.

"I think I will have to travel," Langdale said to his father. "I will go and search for this girl Fairway."

"I advise you to stay here," his father said. "No good will come of this."

It was then that Langdale started to feel alone. His father had no useful advice for him. The other boys in the valley were as young as he was, and none of them knew anything about travelling into the wider world that might help him. Also, they all seemed quite satisfied with life in the valley.

"Why are you still thinking about that giantess?" they said. "Go and get a girl from Marradale." And then they would carry on with their work.

Langdale was sure his mother would have understood better. As he remembered, his mother often had a different perspective on matters, and she had always helped her son with whatever problems he had had. But his mother had died.

One night, all was dark in Langdale, but the boy did not sleep.

This is what he thought: "Is it not true that the dead waken more easily at night? When I have been careless enough to wander close to the barrows at night, I have sensed the dead watching me closely, and have even felt cold fingers on my shoulder. If I am to speak with my mother, tonight would be a good time to do it."

So he lit a torch, and he walked away from the house and up the valley to where the barrows were. Everything was perfectly still. The sky was clear, and the stars were shining bright above him. Beneath his feet, the grass was crisp, and the marshy ground was dry and springy. He followed the riverbed up the valley, and after a few minutes, he had reached the tall barrows that stood there, dark and silent.

Langdale stood amid the barrows, and he called out as loudly as he dared: "Wake up Meregarth, wake up mother. The time has come to help your son". When nothing happened, he called out again, and then a third time.

Then there came a terrible noise of breaking stones, and the earth shook beneath Langdale's feet. Many huge stones must have cracked at that moment, but Langdale could not see where they were. It seemed also that rain had started to fall, though the sky was still as clear as before. And cold white flames flickered up from the tops of the mounds by where he was standing.

Then a voice spoke. Langdale recognised his mother's voice, but it had grown deeper, or more far away.

Meregarth said: "Who has come to wake me, or who has called me forth? May I never lie and rest under the blackest earth?"

Langdale said: "It is your son, Langdale, who has called for your help."

Meregarth said: "What trouble can have found you that is so great that you call on your mother when she is no longer alive?"

Langdale said: "I am cursed, mother. I may get no rest or satisfaction until I have found a certain girl who my eyes have never seen. That maiden is called Fairway, and I don't know where I might find her, only that it is far away from here. It was a giantess who was walking here in the valley who did this to me."

Meregarth said: "Then you must travel. If you stay in this valley, you will live in frustration for as long as you remain alive. But set out with good intentions, and I imagine you will soon find the girl you are longing for. I suppose she lives on an island across the sea. It will not be easy for you to get there, but I will help you if I can. With these gifts I will help you."

As soon as these words were spoken, a horse walked out of the mound. That horse was pale as the tops of the waves that break over the shoals off the sea strand, and it glistened like the moon reflected in the sea.

"This horse is called Waverunner. He runs as easily across the water as across dry land."

Then a purse appeared at the entrance of the mound.

"This purse holds one gold coin. But if you spend the coin and then look again inside the purse, you will see that the coin has returned."

Then a ring appeared at the entrance of the mound.

"This ring may help you if you find the girl. Be good to her and speak well to her if you find her. I cannot help you any more than this."

After that the voice was quiet.

The rain stopped, and the ghost flames on the barrows went out. Langdale saw that his own torch had gone out as well, so he made his way back to the house with the horse and the purse and the ring with nothing more than starlight to show him the way. But he was comforted by this meeting with his mother, and he slept well that night.

The next morning, Langdale saddled up his new horse. He said goodbye to the elder Langdale, and he set off on his quest.

"Listen horse," Langdale said. "If we are to cross the sea, we must first reach the seashore. I have never seen the sea, so I don't know the way there. But from the look of you, you have spent some time in those salt waves. So if you know the way to the sea, lead on."

Waverunner did not follow the valley road down towards Marradale and the lake, but instead he turned up towards the high fells. The land rose up high and steep in front of them, but the surefooted horse found a way through. They climbed higher and higher on a narrow path that led at last to a gap in the mountains. And then just as steeply as they had come up, so they came down until they reached a valley that Langdale had never seen before.

They followed that valley down, alongside a running river, past sunlit woodlands and marshy clearings, past fields of sheep. They left the high fells behind them, and the landscape began to open up. Before too long they had reached the coast, and then the only thing that lay ahead was the wide blue that stretched away further than Langdale could see. It was unlike anything he had seen before.

A breeze blew onto the shore, sticky with salt and full of the scent of seaweed. But even stranger to Langdale was the noise. The air was filled with the mewing of seagulls that wheeled overhead. And waves broke on the shore, rattling the shingle. There were boats there too, pulled up onto the strand.

An old man was sitting on a chair next to the water, and Langdale approached him.

"Is there an island near here that I might find if I go out to sea?" he asked the man.

The old man said: "I don't know whether you want to be taken there, or if you are just asking me to tell you that the place exists. But you should consider this: My whole life is dedicated to knowing this one fact. My whole livelihood comes from telling ambitious young men who pass by here how they might find the island where the castle Highlife stands. Now that you know this, I expect that you can easily persuade me to tell you what you want to know."

"I will persuade you to do it with this coin," Langdale said, and he reached into the purse his mother had given him, and he handed the gold coin to the man.

"It is easy for me to tell you where that island is," the man said, "though I don't know how you plan to get there. The island lies in the west. On a good day you might see it from here, but today is not a good day. Once you are out at sea, head westward, and you will soon see the island in front of you."

So Langdale left the old man behind. Waverunner set off at a gallop down the beach, and when he reached the water the horse did not stop. He ran on across the surface of the sea just as though he had been running on dry land. They rode west, just as the man had told them, and it was not long before the outline of an island appeared ahead of them.

As they approached the island, Langdale saw a wonderful castle. But as they came in closer to the shore, a whole host of cats came running out of holes all along the coast. They were snarling and growling, arching their backs and waving their paws.

"We cannot come in to land here by the castle," Langdale said to his horse. "Not to such a welcome!"

So they went on across the water, following the coastline. As Waverunner rounded a headland, they came to a secluded bay. There was a beach of white sand, and beyond the beach was a flat woodland. Nothing was moving as far as Langdale could see, so they approached the seashore.

They stepped out of the sea and entered the woods. Slender silver birch trees and tall pines stood widely spaced on a carpet of moss and bilberry. The sunlight that came through the leaves was fresh yellow and green. Waverunner picked his way through the trees, and after a few minutes a wide field opened up in front of them. The field was filled with sheep. In the middle of the sheep there was a mound, and on top of the mound there stood an old man with a shepherd's crook. Langdale rode over to speak to him.

Langdale said: "Tell me, shepherd, whose sheep are these, or who is your master?"

The shepherd said: "I will answer this, though it hardly seems right to ride into a foreign land and demand answers to questions without first telling your own name, or why you have come."

Langdale said: "I shouldn't have to tell my name to a shepherd, but I have no reason to hide it from you. My name is Wanderwide. And I have come here to find a certain maiden. Perhaps you could tell me how I might do that."

The shepherd said: "I know of one maiden on this island, and these are her sheep. But I don't know whether she would thank me for helping you find her."

Langdale said: "But I would thank you for it, with this coin." And he took the gold coin from his purse and handed it to the shepherd.

The shepherd said: "The maiden is called Fairway, and she is in a castle here that is called Highlife. Perhaps you saw it as you rode here across the sea."

Langdale said: "I saw that castle, but tell me how I might enter it."

The shepherd said: "It is easy for me to explain how you might enter that castle, but it will be harder for you to do it. The walls of Highlife are built of stone. They are thick and high and sheer. They will be difficult for you to climb, and that horse you are riding will not leap over them. The gate to Highlife is made from the hardest iron and steel, and it is always locked. But if you unlock the castle gate, you will be able to enter."

Langdale said: "Tell me, who has the key to the castle gate, or how can I get it?"

The shepherd said: "I can tell you where that key is, but it will be hard for you to get it. The key is guarded by lions and bears. If you can get those lions and bears to fall asleep, it will be easy for you to go and take the key."

Langdale said: "Tell me, how can I lull the lions and bears to sleep?"

The shepherd said: "I can easily tell you how to do that, but it will be hard for you to carry it out. The lions and bears will all fall asleep as soon as they hear a certain song. Sing that song as you go to them, and you will surely find that they fall asleep at once."

Langdale said: "So tell me, what song is that, or how can I learn it?"

The shepherd said: "I can tell you how you might learn that song, but it will be hard for you to do it. There is a nightingale called Evensong who knows that song. That nightingale sings more sweetly than any other bird. They said she learned her skills in music from Heavenwell herself. That is how she is able to sing such a slumber song. If you find Evensong, you will be able to learn the song."

Langdale said: "Tell me then, where is this nightingale, or how can I find her?"

The shepherd said: "It is easy for me to tell you where Evensong is, but it will be harder for you to find her. She sits on a branch of the great linden tree that grows in the courtyard of the castle Highlife, and there she sings to everyone in the castle. The maiden Fairway is very fond of the nightingale's song, and she sits under that tree often so that she might listen. To find Evensong, you will have to go to that tree."

Langdale said: "It seems that it is difficult to enter Highlife to reach the maiden Fairway."

The shepherd said: "Many have tried to do it, and many have failed. The truth is this: the maiden is waiting for a certain young man to come who her eyes have never seen. That young man's name is Langdale."

Langdale said: "That is interesting for me, because my name is Langdale."

The shepherd said: "That is not what you told me before. I can tell you this: if you are lying to me now, and you try to enter and fail, things will not go well for you. It would be better for you to ride back across the sea on that horse that you rode here on. But if you are telling me the truth and you are this Langdale, you may try to enter."

So Langdale left the shepherd and rode up to the castle. The stone walls rose high in front of him, and the gates were all of iron and steel. Still on his horse, he pushed the gate with his hand. As he did that, the locks fell off that gate and crashed to the ground. The gate swung easily open, and Langdale rode into the castle.

In the middle of the courtyard, there was a great linden tree, and Langdale could hear the sound of birdsong coming from the tree. And under the tree there was a maiden, who stood up as soon as she saw the rider enter the castle.

The maiden said: "What is the meaning of this? Who are you who have dared to enter here, or how did you manage to pass the lions and bears?"

Langdale said: "If you are the maiden Fairway, I have travelled a long way for your sake. I have thought of little else since I first heard about you in the valley where I was born. I could not rest until I found you, and now that I have seen you, I do not plan to leave again. My name is Langdale, and to enter this castle I simply pushed the gate and it opened."

Fairway said: "If you are Langdale, it is good that you have come."

Then Langdale gave her the ring that his mother had given him. The two of them were soon married and they remained at Highlife after that.

The Myth of Blue

Careglad said to her mother: "Tell me about Blue"

Her mother said: "Blue lives at the bottom of a deep depression. That hole is called Swallowhole, though some call it Gloompit. Most people walk about high above him in the bright sunshine. They hardly bother to look down into the hole where Blue is. It is very dark down there.

"The walls of the hole are steep. There are rock faces that are damp and slick due to the lack of sunlight, and the slopes are covered in loose slippery moss. It can be difficult for many people to climb out of there without help.

"Blue has been at the bottom of the hole for so long that he has grown used to the lonely darkness there."

Herder overheard this. He said: "There is more to the story of Blue. Once, he was a fierce warrior. There was no-one braver or more skilled in battle. The songs that were sung then about Blue were rather different from the stories that are told now. I don't suppose anyone remembers those glorious songs. It has been a long time since I heard them sung."

* * *

Once a year, the Elders of Highgarth would send a bowl of soup down to the bottom of the deep hole to Blue. That soup was called Revival, and it was made from nine herbs and fruits that had to be gathered from all across the land. It was prepared in the cookhouse by Simmering, and it was served in a bowl called Ampleful. None of the Elders really wanted to make the difficult trip down into the hole, though they were all fit and well enough to climb down and up with no great problem, even carrying a bowl of hot soup.

One time, Herder was out walking in the sunlit wilderness, with nothing around but the incomprehensible song of invisible birds high above him, and the occasional glimmer of golden sheep scattered across the distant moors. He happened to pass the top of Swallowhole, and he remembered about Blue and the soup. The time when they usually took the soup down to Blue had passed, and it seemed that they had all forgotten all about it.

Some time after that, he returned to Highgarth, and he called all the Elders together. They were all gathered in the great hall, and Herder said:

"I was out walking, and I remembered that no-one has taken the soup to Blue this year. I suppose no-one will step up willingly to take it."

They muttered among themselves, but none of them wanted to do it. So Mindrace brought out the two dice, Lucklander and Fairfaller.

One time, a giant called Longleg had come running out of the fells, screaming wildly and brandishing a huge club above his head. That giant was paying no heed to where he was putting his feet, and he tripped and fell, and as he landed he smashed his skull on a cliff. Lucklander and Fairfaller were carved from the leg bone of that giant, and they were the fairest dice that anyone knew of.

Careglad was there. She had not played the dice game before, but she threw first and threw high. "I don't suppose that score can be beaten," said Mindrace. So no-one else had to throw the dice. Careglad lost the game, and she was chosen to take the soup to Blue.

Simmering made the soup, and he gave it to Careglad in the bowl Ampleful. And away she walked over the moorland until she reached the top of Swallowhole. The descent into the depths of the pit was steep, and as she went down deeper, where there was less sunlight, the rocks grew damp and slippery, and there was more moss on the ground. She had to take great care not to lose her footing.

But Careglad reached the bottom of the hole without dropping the soup, and she called out: "Blue, where are you? I cannot see in this darkness."

Blue replied: "Who has come here to me?"

Careglad said: "It is Careglad who has come. I have brought you the soup in the bowl Ampleful."

Blue said: "I am glad that you have come."

And Careglad gave the soup to Blue, and he ate it up.

Careglad said: "It is bad that you are living all forgotten down here in this hole. I will not forget you again."

Then she climbed out of the hole and returned home.

It was barely a week later when Careglad returned to the hole again, carrying the bowl Ampleful filled with more hot soup. The Elders had not been pleased that Careglad wanted to return so soon with more soup. "Who is going to make the soup?" they grumbled. "And why does he need more soup so soon?"

"If you had not forgotten him down there then maybe he would not be in such a bad way," said Careglad. "I will gladly make the soup myself if someone will show me how to do it."

But Simmering made the soup in the cookhouse, and he gave it to Careglad. And she carried it to the bottom of Gloompit to give to Blue.

When he had eaten the soup, Careglad said: "Come with me. I will help you come out of the hole."

But Blue said to Careglad: "Leave me be. If you ever manage to bring me up out of this hole, you do not know what you will see. Perhaps you like me well enough when I am in this place. But if I were to get out of Gloompit and feel the sunshine on my skin, perhaps my thoughts would not be with you. Perhaps I might remember how things were before. Perhaps I will remember how I used to be."

But Careglad said: "I trust you."

Blue said to Careglad: "It is so dark here. I cannot see you, and you cannot see me. Perhaps if we get out of here, we see each other, and one of us will not like what we see. Perhaps you will not like me as much then."

Careglad said: "I like you very much now. I don't suppose that will change when we are in a more pleasant place."

Blue said to Careglad: "Perhaps the sunlight will change me. You like me well enough as I am now, here in the darkness at the bottom of this hole. But perhaps I will change. I was not always like this. You might not like what I become if I get out of Gloompit and feel the sunshine on my face."

Careglad climbed up and out of Swallowhole and returned to Highgarth, but she did not stay away for long.

The Elders were not pleased when Careglad told them that she meant to take soup to Blue for a third time. "You cannot take more soup down there," they said. "Once a year is enough. Now you want to take it three times in only a few days. Do you not know how much effort it is to make that soup?"

Careglad said: "I imagine I will bring him up out of that awful place, and then none of you will have to take him soup there ever again. You should be happy to hear this as you hate doing it so much."

So they reluctantly agreed, and Simmering handed Careglad a third bowl of soup.

She made her way to the place where the hole was and she descended carefully and slowly into the depths.

"I am happy that you have come back again so soon," said Blue, and he ate the soup.

"I want you to come with me," Careglad said. "You may not find it easy to climb out of this hole, but I will help you, and I think you will make it."

"Very well," said Blue. "Thank you. I would like you to do it."

They held each other tight and close for a long time where they were standing in the darkness, and then they started to climb. Higher they went, and even higher. Careglad helped Blue pass the most difficult parts that he was too weak to pass on his own. Past the moss they climbed, and past the rocks. She gave him her hand. Everything grew less black and more grey, and by the time they emerged into the sunshine, Careglad was pregnant.

They looked at each other as they stood there in the wilderness on the edge of the hole, blinking in the light. They both liked what they saw, and they smiled.

* * *

And that is how the story ends.

And the little boy said: "But that's not the end of the story! It sounds like that was only the beginning for Blue and Careglad. What happened next?"

It is true, it was not the end of Blue or Careglad, but it is the end of this story.

And the little boy said: "But how can the story end when there is so much left to happen? What happened next, or did they live happily ever after, or did they die in the end, or what happened to the baby?"

Those things are not part of this story. Perhaps they are part of another story, or perhaps they are part of many other stories, or perhaps in those other stories Blue and Careglad are known by other names.

They didn't die in this story, and they have still not died, for as long as this story is told and retold, they are kept alive. And no matter what happened next, Blue is still the great warrior who was somehow lost and who found himself in a deep hole. And Careglad is still the one who was able to help him out of there.

The Allure of Heft, part I

One time, Heave was away, and Mindrace paid his daughter Heft a visit. Mindrace and Heft were lying in the hall in Oakwood, gazing up at the leafy roof. This is what they said:

Heft said to Mindrace: "Many giants chase me. I am repulsed by them, and yet also I find them fascinating. The wisdom of those giants astonishes me. I wonder whether any of them will ever catch me."

Mindrace said to Heft: "I know of one giant. His name is Heftnetter. He is the wisest of them all. I have heard of few who are wiser than him. If any of them will catch you, I imagine it will be him. But he does not dare to come to you. He sits under a rock and waits. Perhaps he thinks that it will be you and not him who will take the lead, and that you will seek him out."

Heft said to Mindrace: "I find it delightful that there is a very wise giant who sits under a rock, thinking great thoughts. How wonderful that he thinks about me so much."

Mindrace said to Heft: "I sense that Heftnetter is not as wise as he thinks if he believes he will win you in this way. The giants know that you are strong, and that few women are stronger. But they know little else about your character. I think it is safe to say that Heftnetter does not know you as well as I do."

And then Heft laughed. Her laugh was as sweet-sounding as birdsong, and as tuneful as a plucked harp. The leaves on the trees in Oakwood trembled as she laughed, and the ground shook beneath her body where she lay.

The Allure of Heft, part II

Two giants were sitting high in the mountains alongside a teardrop tarn, deep and dark.

The sun hung half-obscured by a high ridge, and the fading light played over the huge boulders that littered the slopes. Some of them seemed to move, while unseen ears listened to what was said.

"I have heard," said one, "that Heave is away. He has wandered off to look for a fight. I am sure his daughter is left behind in Oakwood. Now might be a good time to pay her a visit, for she is surely very beautiful."

"They call me Reckless," said the other. "But even I do not dare to walk into Oakwood, whether Heave is away or not. Even if he is away, he may come back."

"They call me Bolder," said the other. "I will go myself. There is no way I would miss out on this chance."

So that very night, Bolder came down from the mountains and walked in the valley where the oak trees were. He passed beyond the lake that fills the lower part of that valley, and he walked into the woods. As he passed through the oak trees, his head was above the leafy treetops, so he had to take care where he was putting his feet. It was not long before he reached Heave's hall.

When he saw the huge hall, held up by pillars the size of tree trunks, the giant grew a little apprehensive, even though he would have to stoop low to enter.

But having come so far, and with a chance to see the famous Heft, he overcame his fear. Bolder bent and tapped on the hall door.

It was not long before the door of the hall swung open. But the giant was taken aback, for it was not the girl Heft who stood there, and neither was it her father Heave. It was another of the Elders, perhaps even more powerful.

Half dressed, tucking his shirt into his trousers, holding his grey coat under his arm, it was the unmistakeable figure of Mindrace.

But Mindrace was just as surprised. He hardly expected to see a giant knocking on the door of the hall at Oakwood.

"Yes, the girl is here," Mindrace said. "But I don't think she will see you. She is rather occupied."

Bolder said: "I have come a long way for her sake. It would be a shame for me to turn around and return home now, having come this far. They say you know many things. If you can answer my riddles then I will go home. But if you cannot answer then you should let me pass."

Mindrace said: "You may ask me your riddles, but I also have some riddles that I will ask you."

Bolder said: "You may ask me whatever you want, and I will answer if I can."

Mindrace said: "Tell me then, Bolder, if you know. Who was it who murdered that dwarf as he lay in his bed one night? Who was Sleepy's killer, according to the old lore?"

Bolder said: "This I know well. Day it was who crept in at the window. The dwarf had no chance against his flashing blade. Dawn-ray is that sword's name, forged by the great Smith in Micklewood. I know few swords that are sharper or lighter, or that can be swung faster through the air.

"They say you know many things, but tell me, who is this: They called you the fairest, the girl dressed in red. With sharp spears, you were eager. You stabbed any man who dared come near. Be careful, young one: after a brief summer your looks will fade."

Mindrace said: "That is not hard to answer. The girl is a rose, blushing pink. Many hands are reddened on her thorns.

"Tell me then, Bolder, if you know. Who sowed the seeds of discord at Highgarth? Who caused the secrets to be spoken out loud?"

Bolder said: "This I know well. Mead it was who walked naked through the gates, saying nothing would be hidden. That giantess holds great power over men's minds. To some, she whispers memories, over others, she breathes forgetfulness. Mead invites all men to speak the truth, and many forget that some things are better left unsaid.

"They say you know many things, but tell me, who is this: I come ahead of a great light. I am not the light, but far and wide I wander to tell about the light. And all who see me may know about the light. I am dark, imprecise, diffuse. I am unlike that light, but without me he is never seen."

Mindrace said: "That is not difficult, the answer is blown like smoke, for there is no fire without it.

"Tell me then, Bolder, if you know. Who is Heave's great enemy? Who is it who will prove a match for his strength?"

Bolder said: "This I know well. To look at her you would not think it, for she looks as frail and fragile as a grandmother. Her touch is light, but she moves slowly forward, and she will never stop. Her name is Age, and for all his strength, he cannot beat her.

"They say you know many things, but tell me, who is this: Shaped by chilly breaths, you grew, hard and bright as adamant, but a delicate and fragile wonder. You sparkle in the sunshine, and your strength fades. From water you came, and to water you will return."

Mindrace said: "This riddle I know, the answer is cold ice, that glistens in the warm sun, and melts to water.

"Tell me then, Bolder, if you know, how did the dragon come to be? Who was it who made that magic, who was it who cast the spell? Whose was the cursed gold that Goldeneye stole?"

Bolder said: "I cannot be tricked by this riddle. There was no great curse. The gold that Goldeneye gathered came from many places. That man saw gold and more gold. His head was turned, his eyes were bright. Every golden coin adds up, and every ring and golden cup. How often he turned tail, how often he fled, the gold he grasped clutched at his chest. Many little curses called after him. Many small things add up to something bigger. That is the true tale of how Goldeneye became what he is today.

"They say you know many things, but tell me, who is this: I plough a path in a snowy field, leaving my mark in untouched ground. I am mightier than I may seem. Dark furrows I left there, crooked, winding, swirling, black, and the meaning clear for many men to see."

Mindrace said: "This riddle is not hard to answer. It is a pen, writing letters on a page so men may later know the meaning.

"Tell me then Bolder, if you know, who does Heave fear the most?"

Bolder said: "This I know well. Fathers are finally beaten by their sons, and pupils will surpass their teachers. He fears he will be beaten by a younger man, even if he has no sons himself. He fears that a younger man will take his daughter, and that he will be unable to prevent it. He fears that he will be unable to protect her, even though she neither wants nor needs his protection.

"They say you know many things, but tell me, who is this: I wander lonely, homeless and exiled. My beard is grey, often my colour shifts. There is no place on this earth for me. My tears drench the world, everywhere you see is soaked with my sorrows."

Mindrace said: "Now you try to be too clever, but you show yourself instead to be foolish. It is not so clever to taunt your opponent when he is a stronger man, or when you are in another man's house."

Bolder said: "You have misunderstood me. This was not the meaning of the riddle. The answer is in the clouds above."

Mindrace said: "I see you know many things, but there are still some things that you miss. You may think that you have won this contest, but you will soon see things differently. If I look up now, I can see the clouds. I can see the sky turning grey. I can hear the chattering of the little birds, telling me that day is coming. But I can see this for myself. Night is gone, and darkness has fled away. Heft is here in the hall, but you will never see her. The rising sun will strike you down, and there will be new crags and boulders here in this valley today."

The Lone Pine

I know of a tree. It stands alone on a mountainside. Many times I have walked past that tree, or I have seen it on the horizon. It stands as a waymarker, and when I pass by that place, I know where I am or which way I should walk or how far it is to the farm in the valley below.

One time I was walking that way on the moor and mountain. The cloud was low, and I couldn't see far. I came to a place where I thought I would see the tree, but the tree was not there. I wandered back and forth across that mountainside, searching for the place where the tree stood, so that I could drop down and reach the farm. I thought I must have taken a wrong turning, because I never saw that tree.

Later, I was out walking on that same mountain, and I saw the tree, and I said: "When I was walking here in bad weather I couldn't find you, and I couldn't find my way."

The tree said: "Once, a great forest stood here. That was many years ago. I am not old enough to remember that forest myself, but I have heard stories told about it.

"All year long I stand alone here on the mountainside, and all is well. I could not wish for a better place to stand. And yet sometimes I find myself longing for something. I cannot say whether it is something I have lost, or something that I imagine I might have lost, but that I never really had. I long to be surrounded by other trees, by others like me. I long for community, or to lose myself among countless others.

"And so sometimes, not often, not usually more than once a year, and only for a few days, I will leave this place. And I will go to one of the great forests that still stand in this land. Micklewood is one, Greywood is another. I will not stay there long, just long enough to be reminded of our civilisation, of the great community of trees.

"The way I experience the world is different when I am surrounded by other trees. Even the weather feels different in the forest. Here on the moor, I am blown by the wind from the southwest. Always it comes from there, and I do not resist. I bend with it. But in the forest we are many, and when the wind blows I hardly feel the full force of it. I hear the whispering in the tops of all the trees together. There are so many trees there, and so tall. It feels like the rain falls more lightly in the forest. Even when a storm rages there is some comfort in being surrounded by others who are feeling that same storm.

"But a few days in the forest is enough for me. And then I return to this place on the high fell, the views, the weather, the solitude.

"So if you came this way and I was not here, I may have been in Micklewood. Or maybe you had just lost your way in the mist."

The Straw Man

The days are long in summertime, but even summer days come to an end. It may be late when the sun sinks low, and the land is freed from its glare, though the sky remains clear and bright. And creatures that have been sheltering from the heat all day long can come out at last into the evening.

Two giants sat by the shore of a long lake. One of them was called Broadhead, and he said: "I have heard that Heave has been seen in our lands again. Again I have heard of his swinging club. Again, stories of cracked shin bones of giants who happened to walk his way, or cracked skulls of giants sleeping peacefully on the ground where he passed."

The other was called Hardnose, and he said: "He wanders ever wider."

* * *

Heave lives in Oakdale. He has a high hall that stands in the woods called Oakwood that lie above the lake Overwater. The roof of that hall is as high as the leafy canopy of the woods, held up by tall oak trunks. It is a sheltered place in that wet valley.

But as he sat in Oakdale, Heave was not content. He found his mind turning more and more to thoughts of the threats posed by giants. At that time, the giants mostly sat in the north or in the east, though Heave was well aware that any number of them could appear at any time from any direction.

Heave had grown so furious at the thought of the giants that one day he decided he would have to walk to the stronghold at Highgarth to discuss this matter with Mindrace. It is not too far from Oakdale to Highgarth. Or it is not too far for a bird to fly. But these places both lie in the high fells, so a straight-line route is blocked by steep climbs, boulder fields, and impassable rock faces. On foot, a traveller must follow the lines of the landscape, up valleys, though gaps in the mountains, and down into new areas that open up on the far side. But the ground is rough, the paths are indistinct.

The Oakdale river meanders dark and wide through the woodlands as it flows down towards the lake Overwater. But this river is made up of the coming together of fast-flowing white-water streams that rush down into the valley from the mountains above. Wildcat Gill is one. Sourmilk Gill is another. Henside Gill is another. There are more streams that flow off the fells and tumble through the trees.

As Heave set off, he followed the stream called Sourmilk Gill up and out of the valley. He left the trees behind, and he reached a large flat-topped ridge, tussocky and marshy underfoot. There were small tarns there, dark and deep, and rocky summits stood spaced out along that ridge like deserted watchtowers. Close to these tops, the ground was drier, but in the lower parts in between, it grew wetter again. The trudge along that wide ridge seemed to take a long time.

There were sheep on the fell, but those sheep hardly seemed bothered by the wandering figure. They carried on grazing on the marshy ground. And all this time, he could hear the chatter of small birds overhead, somewhere out of sight. Heave could hardly see whether those birds had been following him all the way from Oakdale. Or whether it was so many different little birds, each staying on their own patch, and passing on their messages in their own language.

The ridge was high, but it was surrounded by higher fells in many shapes. He passed by a valley far below him where he could see the vast marsh called Bleamire. At last, Heave reached a col where he could drop down into another valley. He followed that winding valley around past cliffs and boulders, and soon he had reached the magnificent walls of Highgarth, where he hoped he would find Mindrace.

* * *

The walls shone. High and impenetrable. Heave walked through the open gate. The great tree stood in the courtyard. The fires of home were burning in the hearths.

But when Heave walked through the door of the great hall at Highgarth, he stopped in horror. Mindrace was there all right, sitting in the high chair. But there, seated across from him (Heave could barely believe it) was the unmistakeable figure of a giant.

"How can this be?" he thundered. "Are we inviting giants into our halls now? Have they entered the very heart of everything we hold dear, or everything we need to protect? How many times have you called on me to defend us from the chaos of the giants?"

"This giant is my guest," said Mindrace. "He is among the wisest of beings."

"I declare I never saw a wise giant in my life," said Heave. "This is the proof: I don't know of anyone who has fought more giants or trolls than I have. They are always very stupid. I just take a swing with my club, and with one firm strike they often crumble into rubble." To the giant, Broadhead, he said: "You look just like one of those trolls. I cannot imagine you know anything worth knowing, or can say anything worth hearing."

Then Heave said: "I came here to Highgarth today with one thing in mind. I came to ask Mindrace's advice about the problem we have – the problem of the giants."

Mindrace said to Heave: "It is good that you came here to ask this today. Maybe we will be able to find a solution."

Broadhead said to Heave: "I can suggest one thing: It would be good if we were not subject to your constant attacks."

Heave said: "Oh, so then the giants would be free to overrun this land!"

Broadhead said: "I see we are not going to resolve this through discussion. Will you fight then? Against me, or against a champion who we have chosen?"

"No-one ever dared challenge me to a duel before," said Heave. "But why not fight me here and now? Do you think I will allow you to freely walk out of here back to your own land?"

"There is not much honour in fighting an unarmed man," said Mindrace. "If you are going to fight, why not agree on a time and place to do it?"

And so the arrangements were made, and they agreed that the duel would be held at the meeting place between Broadwater and Overwater, where the Oakdale river joins the Roaring river. Between the three peaks of Trollfell and Bleaberry Fell and Little Bell.

* * *

The giants sat beside the lake, and they wondered how they might solve their predicament.

Highbrow said: "Let him have his victory. He will not leave us be unless he is satisfied. The victory must be a great one."

Hardnose said: "And who is prepared to go out and meet him?"

Broadhead said: "None of us need to do that. There is no need for any of us to feel the crack of his club against our shins. Or to feel our heads crumble to rubble. There is another way for us to seem to lose this fight, and none of us need to get hurt. We can build a huge man, the figure of a champion. We can build him so he stands taller than any of us, reaching up into the sky. When Heave knocks that dummy down, he will surely believe he has won a great victory."

So the giants gathered as much straw as they could find, and they set about making an enormous figure in the form of a man. They wove and tied the straw in bundles, and they bound it together with mud that they scraped from the bottom of the lake. They set big red stones in his head for eyes. And when the work was finished, Hardnose breathed into the mouth of the thing that they had made, and he was alive.

"Your name is Mudleg," said Broadhead. "Now stand up. Heave is coming soon, and you will be our champion to fight against him."

That straw man was so huge that when he stood up, he could easily stand astride the lake, and his head reached up to the felltops and the clouds.

* * *

The time came for the duel, and Heave came walking with his club. He was expecting to see the giant, Broadhead. But instead he saw the giant straw man standing astride the lake. He saw the red stones that he had for eyes, and how they seemed to glow red when the sunlight glinted against them. And Heave was at once filled with fury. He let out a war cry, and he rushed towards the straw man. But the straw man was so big that Heave had been quite far away when he had first seen it, so it took him some time to reach it, even though he was running hard.

The straw man didn't know what to do. He could feel Heave striking blows against his right leg and ankle. But he didn't know what was happening, and he couldn't move his feet. He just stood there, swaying. Perhaps it was his own attempts to move his unaccustomed limbs that made him sway. Perhaps he was swaying in the breeze that was blowing down the valley and over the lake. Perhaps the vibrations of being hit in the leg by a big oak club were causing him to sway. Or perhaps, as Heave would tell later, the giant was so afraid that he simply stood there, trembling.

Straw and mud flew from the straw man's shins and calves with every blow that Heave struck. He became less and less stable, and he started to wobble more and more. Soon the straw man's leg cracked, and he came tumbling down out of the sky and landed in the lake. As Mudleg's body hit the water, a great wave rose up.

Water flowed out of the lake and rushed across the flat land that lies between Broadwater and Overwater, and it seemed for a while that the two had joined into one much greater lake. Much of the surrounding land was flooded, and Broadhead's own halls were filled with water.

* * *

And is it cruel to create a living thing, knowing that it too will surely die, or knowing that its only purpose in the world would be to be knocked down?

Maybe it would have been different if the man the giants made had not been so like one of them. There are those in the world who have a passion for creation. It is often seen as a talent, that everything they make seems alive. It might perhaps be thought of as a curse.

Hunter's Arrival in Yewdale

When Hunter first came to the land, he did not have a hall or anywhere to live. He passed through many places, and at last he came to a valley where many yew trees were growing. For that reason it was called Yewdale.

The lower part of the valley was narrow, and a stream tumbled swiftly down through steep woodlands of oak and ash. The stream splashed against so many rocks that it looked more like milk than water. But higher up, the valley grew broad and flat-bottomed. It was surrounded on all sides by high fellsides that rose up abruptly like steep walls. There, the stream meandered slowly through the flat grassland, and the valley bottom was marked only by the many single yew trees that gave the valley its name, and also by a few boulders of enormous size that must have fallen from the fells above.

"This would be a good place to live," thought Hunter.

He walked over to one of the yew trees. "This branch would be perfect for a new bow," he thought to himself. He couldn't wait. The branch was soon in his hands, and he was working it with a knife.

He didn't see the movement at first. One of the boulders that had been sitting on the valley bottom shivered and then stood up to its full height. It was a troll woman, or a giantess. When Hunter saw her, he leapt up at once. That giantess was dark-haired, and the air seemed to grow chilly around her. She was undoubtedly beautiful, with skin like smooth stone, but her face was all indignation and disbelief.

"Who are you, or why have you cut one of the yew trees?" she said.

"I have no reason to conceal my name from you," he said, "but I am surprised that you ask me my name without telling me your own. As for the tree, you may know that yew wood makes an excellent hunting bow, and that is what I am making."

The giantess was furious at this response. "I am astonished that you refuse to tell me your name. You should know that I am Shadow, and this valley is Yewdale, and this is my home. Perhaps if you are so ill-mannered, I should not be surprised that you took a branch from that tree without asking."

"I am surprised to hear you say that this is your home," said Hunter. "I have decided that I will live here myself, and I will soon build a hall in this very spot. I don't suppose you will stay here very long after that. I can also tell you that my name is Hunter, though I am surprised you didn't know that already."

"Intolerable!" cried Shadow. "I suggest you leave here at once."

"Well I have no intention of leaving," he said.

And the two of them stood facing one another in speechless indignation.

Shadow blinked. She let out a scream that echoed from fell wall to fell wall and back again, all around that valley. "Very well. You can live in this place," she cried. "But I don't suppose you will enjoy life here for very long." And with that, she turned and fled up into the cliffs and boulders. The rocks moved and cracked where she put her feet, and Hunter could hear the rumbling of great stones shifting high above him for some time after that.

The fells around Yewdale were high, and the valley was deep. So the shadows of the mountains often lay over the house that Hunter built in Yewdale.

* * *

Shadow scowled from the rocks, while Hunter slept in the hall he had built in the valley bottom. They barely spoke. And things went on like that for some time.

One day, Hunter went out with his bow. For most of that day, everything was quiet, and nothing was moving but the birds in the trees. But as time drew on to evening, he came across a boar. The boar was cornered, and there was no way for it to get away. Hunter was sure that he would be able to get the boar with his bow and arrow, but that is not what happened. The boar turned, and it ran at Hunter through the trees. He hardly had time to react. The boar hit him with its sharp tusks. Hunter was badly wounded in his leg. The boar didn't wait. It saw its chance to escape and it was gone.

Hunter made his way back to Yewdale as best he could. It was difficult, as he could hardly walk because of the wound in his leg.

Shadow was in Yewdale when Hunter arrived back at his hall. She had seen him approach, but she hardly knew it was him. He looked different, as he could hardly walk.

She came down to the hall that Hunter had built, and she said to him: "I see that you are badly wounded, and that your wounds are bleeding hard. Let me help you. I will bind your wounds, and after that you should rest here."

And Shadow bound his wounds with cloth, and she healed him as best she could.

Hunter said: "I am badly hurt. I can neither walk nor stand unless these wounds get better."

Shadow said: "There is a healing drink that I can give you. But I fear you may find it very bitter, or hard to swallow."

So she collected fresh herbs, and she mixed the drink. She went to where Hunter was lying, and she said to him: "Drink this, and stay here with me."

She came to him every day and tended his wounds. It took some time, but Hunter's wounds were healed. And he said to Shadow: "You put a lot of care into healing me. I feared this would be my death."

* * *

After all this had happened, Hunter and Shadow were not on such bad terms. They saw each other most days in Yewdale, and it was not long before they decided that they would get married. So they both stayed in Yewdale, and there was much gladness on both sides.

The Boar Hunt

The hall at Applegarth is a great wonder. Applegarth lies in a part of the country where the rainfall is high, but it is also often sunny late into the evening. This makes it a good place for growing fruit, and that was one reason the Lady Fairhair chose that place to build her hall. The great hall at Applegarth is both long and high. The roof is gently curved, higher in the middle, with ornamented gable ends. Viewed from the side, it resembles an upturned ship. Or, bearing in mind the events of this story, its shape could be compared to a hog's back, or a boar lying sleeping. Behind that great hall there are other smaller buildings set around a courtyard. But the wonder of Applegarth, the thing that it is known for, is not the hall itself, but the surrounding apple trees.

The orchard acres are beautiful all year round. At the start of the autumn, the trees are heavy with fruit, sweet and juicy, orange and rosy and green. Those are the harvest days when the fruit is at its freshest, gathered from the trees.

But the most beautiful time is in the spring, when apple blossom covers the trees. A cloud of white bursts forth, appearing all at once like a morning mist to surround and engulf the great hall, hiding it almost completely behind the trees. The scent of apple blossom fills the air. It is a sign of new life and new beginnings, or a reminder that warmer weather is on the way after the harsh emptiness of winter. But just as that beauty so suddenly appears, a fortnight later it is gone. For nothing lasts for ever.

* * *

One day, the gardeners came running to the hall at Applegarth. They asked to see Fairhair, and this is what they said: "Lady, the apple orchards are like our gardens. We tend the trees in your honour, and every year they bring forth fruit. But now something awful has happened. There is a terrible boar outside. It has shaken the leaves from the trees, and knocked the unripe fruit onto the ground."

Herder was also there at Applegarth. He said: "I know that boar. It is a magical boar. The boar is black, yet its bristles glow. It can run as fast as any hound, and it rarely gets tired. That boar is called Torch."

So they went outside, and the boar was standing there, big and dark. Fairhair said to the boar: "What have you done? Or why have you done this?"

The boar said:

> Apple trees grow here,
> Many things bear fruit.
> Ideas can grow faster than leafless trees,
> They survive without water or sunlight,
> Growing by the power of thought alone.
> Have you forgotten about shame,
> Or how it feels to walk in infamy?
> Where is your lover now,
> Or why have you abandoned him?
> Better not to talk so loud,
> When the truth escapes, it will run,
> Faster than a fleeing boar,
> Or faster than the wind.

And as it spoke, the apple trees shook, and the leaves fell to the ground.

* * *

I know of another great wonder, and that is the tree at Yewdale. There is a hall in Yewdale close to that tree, and Hunter built that hall.

That great tree is the oldest of all the trees. It is taller than most other trees, and it has a wider trunk. Its bark is rough, and it is rooted fast in the earth. It seems as though that tree has stood there since the beginning of time. It spreads its branches wide. And it stands ever green, never shedding its needles, constant in the heat of summer, and deeply green all through the snowy winter.

One day the boar came crashing into Yewdale. It ran up the valley from the lake, following the chattering stream through the woods. It was easy to see which way that boar had run, as it left only destruction and despair behind it. Many trees were knocked down, and the ground was churned to mud. The boar came to the place where the valley widened out, where the yew trees were, and where Hunter's hall stood.

Hunter came out to see what was happening, and he saw where the boar stood, big and dark.

The boar said:

> Have you forgotten who made this place,
> Or who formed the world you live in?
> What did you say when he came knocking?
> You took something for yourself,
> But did you help when he came looking?
> Should it be so hard to find
> A place in creation?

The words echoed around the mountain walls, and rocks broke and slid, and some narrow paths into the fells behind Yewdale became too unsafe to walk after that.

* * *

The boar ran to the sea coast, and it followed the shore all the way around the country from the south, along the west coast, to the north. The boar ran as fast as the wind, and it left only destruction in its wake from the words it spoke.

Soon the boar came to the muddy sands in the north where Solway sat, watching the water. The peace and calm was disturbed as the boar approached. Its breath was heavy, its hooves thundered against the ground. Many geese that had been standing at the water's edge flew up into the air, honking and barking, and loudly beating their wings.

Solway stood up, and the boar stopped and faced her.

The boar said:

> Answer me this: where is your child now?
> Who taught him what he knows,
> Or who told him what to do?
> If you had called for the strong guard,
> Things would have been different.
> What bigger threat did you expect,
> To come out of the water?
> What could have been bigger than that giant?
> You could not defend against him.

Waves rose up from that calm sea, and broke on the shore.

* * *

The boar ran on the high fells, along grassy ridges above deep valleys. Wherever that boar passed, the grass turned to mud. Heathery slopes burned away. Birds leapt up from the ground in panic. Rocks slid down into the valleys below.

It could run faster than any horse, and it was hardly slowed down when it had to cross a fell that rose up in its path, or when it had to run through a river, or through any forest. And the golden glow from its bristles meant that the boar could see and be seen wherever it went, even as it ran through the darkest night, or through the shadows beneath the fells, or through the woods. Around its neck the boar wore a golden ring. The ring showed that it was the king of all boars.

The boar ran across an upland heath until it came to a long house where Herder lived. Herder was standing outside by the door as the boar approached.

The boar said:

> Many golden sheep roam the fells,
> You say you own them all.
> Have you forgotten who fathered them,
> Or how you came by that ram?
> Did you ever ponder that farmer's fate?
> Favoured by dwarfs, gifted with gold,
> Unfairly deceived.
> You have done well to gain,
> From ill-gotten beginnings.

* * *

The boar visited others of the Elders. It never had anything good to say, and it cared little about the devastation it left behind. The news about the boar spread quickly. And the Elders gathered in Highgarth so that they could discuss what could be done.

Another great wonder is the tree at Highgarth. That tree was not there when Highgarth was built. The Elders had it planted, though they did not plant it themselves. That tree was planted by a wanderer who came as a guest to Highgarth one time. They say that as long as that tree stands, the Elders will be safe in their land.

Herder said: "We have all heard about this boar. It is a magnificent thing to look at. It is big and black and sleek, with sharp tusks. Its eyes are bright, and it runs faster than most other animals. Also the bristles that cover its skin are poisoned. They say that boar is called Torch."

Some of those who had not yet been attacked directly were less easily convinced that anything needed to be done at all.

"There is no boar," they said.

"That is not so," Fairhair said. "The boar is real. Its sharp tusks are not imaginary. Its size is enormous. It runs faster than you may believe. Its existence cannot be denied."

Heave said: "You may believe you saw a boar, but that was no boar. One of the giants has taken on the form of a boar. He means to terrorise us. He means to destroy the fruit trees and the fields of grain that we have grown. Instead of these good crops, he aims to sow discord, and he hopes it will grow into something worse. That boar should be struck down."

Blossom said: "Do you think only of fighting and destruction?"

Heave said: "We have made a good life for ourselves here. We have built something precious. And that is worth protecting from those who want to destroy us. It is not my choice to fight that boar. The boar chose to come here, it chose to harm us, and it chose to try to destroy everything we have made. It is only right that we should defend ourselves."

Fairhair said: "If something stands out as rare and beautiful, it is a great wonder, and we should not allow it to be destroyed. It is worth protecting, and worth defending. For there are those who choose to destroy beautiful things, and there are others who go along with what they are told, and join in with the destruction, even though things will end up worse for them."

Blossom said: "But if what the boar says is true, who are we to say that it should be silenced?"

Herder said: "The boar says it speaks the truth. But that boar also forgets many other things that are also true, or it chooses not to speak them. It chooses to speak only those truths that it knows will bring harm. It remains silent about the glory of the place we have built here. For this place is surely a wonder. There is one more thing that no-one has mentioned: that boar chooses not to speak the truth about itself."

* * *

And so they agreed that they would have to hunt the boar, and the question then arose as to who would do it.

Hunter had come to Highgarth from his home in the Yewdale fells, and he had his bow and arrows with him. He said: "I am the most skilled huntsman here, sure-sighted with the bow, shooting the swiftest arrows. It will be easy for me to track this boar. I will hunt alone."

Mindrace said: "You should not underestimate this boar. It will be difficult for you to catch it. And if you hunt alone, it may kill you before you kill it."

But Hunter was determined that he should be the one to hunt the boar, and that he should use the methods he was accustomed to. So he set off. It was not difficult to track the boar. Wherever it had been, crops and grass were flattened. Trees had shed leaves and twigs, and in some cases whole branches had come off, or trunks were broken. Hunter followed the trail of destruction until at last he saw where the huge boar was standing.

Hunter did not hesitate. He reached for an arrow from his quiver, and he shot it towards the boar. The arrows shot from that bow fly further and faster than any other arrows. But the boar was faster. When it saw the arrow coming towards it, it turned and ran. And although the arrow flew after the boar for some time, it fell to the earth on the flattened ground where the boar had run.

"That is certainly a fast boar," said Hunter.

When Hunter saw that he would not be able to shoot the boar, he returned to Highgarth.

Mindrace said: "If the boar is too fast, there is one way you can slow it down. It is hard to run fast in deep snow. Drive the boar into the snow fields in the high fells. That way it will not be able to run as fast, and your arrows will more easily find their mark."

Hunter set off again to track the boar. It was easy to see where the boar had been, but harder to catch up with it. Winter had come, and snow lay deep on the higher ground. The boar had wandered into one of the long valleys, deep and steep sided. There were ways out of that valley, but each of them involved climbing to a pass or a gap, and each of those passes was well above the snowline. So Hunter followed the boar into the valley.

When the boar Torch saw that Hunter had come, it turned and ran away as fast as it could. The boar ran into a snowfield at full tilt. The boar's feet sank into the snow, which grew deeper and deeper. Soon it was difficult for the boar to run. It struggled to keep moving forward through the untouched snow. It slowed down a lot, and eventually it came to a standstill.

Hunter followed the track the boar had made. The snow had been completely flattened, and it was easy to see where the boar had gone. At last, he saw the creature close up. It seemed huge as it stood motionless in the snow ahead of him. Its back resembled a long and rounded hill, overgrown with bristles. Its tusks were sharp as polished steel. Its watery eyes were dark and deep. That boar was dark, and yet it also glowed. Hunter had heard it roar before, but now it was quiet, and its head shuddered as it let out heavy breaths. But the worst was what came from its awful jaws: surprising words, whispered loudly. This was a dreadful boar.

The boar said: "I shine the torch of truth."

Hunter said: "It may be that you choose to shine a light on certain truths. You are careful to choose what you speak and what you leave unsaid. It is not the whole truth you are telling."

The boar said: "Truth is a strong foundation. Anything built on lies is bound to fall."

Hunter said: "You say you speak the truth, but you are worse than any one of us. You are driven by hate. You have no wish to build anything, or to preserve any of the wonder in the world. You think only of destruction. All that drives you is the thought of how you might destroy all that is right and good and beautiful. We will all die in the end. The difference between us is how we live before that happens. Some of us hope to build beauty. We hope it may outlive us, and we believe it is worth defending. I see nothing in what you are doing beyond jealousy and bitterness. But it seems your time here is nearing its end."

Hunter reached for an arrow. But the boar Torch turned, and with great speed it rushed back through the snow along the way it had already come. The snow had been trampled flat there, so it was not deep, and the boar did not come slowly. Snow flurries flew up into the air on all sides as Torch ran. Before Hunter could fit an arrow to his bowstring, the boar was upon him. Its tusks went through his heart and his belly, and soon the snow was red with blood.

* * *

When the news of Hunter's death reached Highgarth, all the Elders rode out at a gallop. They made a fearsome sight, calling out, and swearing to avenge their fallen kinsman.

They rode out through the weather with grey Mindrace at their head. The hounds ran with them as well: Ruby and Fury, Royal and Merriman. They made swift progress, but the boar Torch was faster. That magic boar always heard them coming, and it moved on more quickly than they could imagine. They passed by many places where they had heard the boar had been. Grisedale and Swinside, Grisebeck and Swindale, and Hogswood and Hogs Earth and Great Boar Fell, and many other places. Often they felt the wind and the rush of the air where the boar had run, but wherever they rode, they never caught sight of that boar.

And in the end, that boar ran into the sea. There was a headland there, projecting into the sea in the south. And that place is called Boars Head even now.

But even as the Elders returned to Highgarth, there was some doubt as to what had happened to the boar. "Perhaps that boar has run out into the sea," some of them said. "I don't believe anyone saw the boar run into the sea," others replied. "More likely it is still waiting, out of sight." They rode out again many times after that to try to find the boar Torch, but they never saw it again.

A Weather Change

One day, Robin decided that he would go out and run through all the land. So he turned himself into a fox, and he ran. He ran across purple-heather moorlands, past sweet-smelling gorse bushes. He ran through Greywood, a red streak under the silent trees. He leapt over tumbling gills and dark rocky pools, and he reached the high tops of many mountains. Sometimes it rained, and sometimes it cleared for a while before it started raining again. It was wet, it was slippery, and the landscape was just as it is on a wet day, with clouds veiling the views, then pulling back.

In the north, the fells were quieter. A river flowed in the bottom of a long treeless valley, and the fox leapt across. The next ridge he ran over was smooth and grassy, but rising up on the ridge top were several oddly shaped rocks that could almost be ancient statues, carved by giants in long-forgotten times, and left to crumble on the wild mountainside. Perhaps long ago this place had been different, less deserted, less faraway. Or perhaps those boulders could have once been trolls, frozen still as stones where they stood.

But as the fox sniffed around the base of one of the stone pillars, the stones turned, and something that must have been an arm reached down to where the fox was. Robin leapt back in alarm. He turned to run, but he had strayed off his path and into a marsh, and he saw that his way was blocked by standing water. He couldn't see a way through. The fox hesitated at the water's edge, and a stony hand closed around his back. Robin found himself lifted up and looking into the awful face of a giant. For those stones were not carved or crumbling, or long forgotten. They were still very much alive.

"There is something about this fox," said the giant. And he looked into the fox's eyes. Those eyes shimmered with a touch of something indescribable, otherworldly. "You are not a fox at all. You are a shape-shifter. A colour-changer. I know well who you are."

The fox remained silent.

Another of the stone pillars moved, and a giant's voice called over: "What have you got there, Broadhead?"

"It looks like a fox, but I don't believe it is a fox," the first giant said.

At that moment it started to rain again.

The giant said: "What weather! We live in a beautiful land, but the weather is bad. Fine days are few. Every day there is wind and rain, often there is a cold that makes us huddle on the hillside. Or there is hail, or snow, or mist."

Robin had been silent, but he had been listening to what the giants were saying. And he had thought of a plan. "What weather!" he said.

Broadhead said: "It speaks! I hardly thought when I first saw you running across the moors that you would be a talking fox. But of course, you are not a fox at all."

The fox said: "It hardly matters who I am. But if you let me go then I will help you."

Broadhead said: "If you help me, I will let you go, though I hardly know what help you could give me.

The fox said: "Many people think about how things could be better in the world."

Broadhead said: "I don't want to change the world. I am not so weak that I dream about this. I look within myself. I make myself the best I can be, so that I may live well within the world. If I tried to change the world, I would surely fail. And even if I succeeded in changing what I wanted to change, who knows what else might also change? Even if I succeeded, many other things could change for the worse."

The fox said: "I heard you talking about the weather. Often people complain that the weather is bad, but I know how you might change it."

Broadhead said: "The weather changes a lot. In the summer it is warmer, in the winter it is colder. That is the way of things. Many days it will rain. It is not so pleasant to be out in the rain, but without it, many things would die. Most days it will also stop raining. Sometimes the wind is strong, sometimes there is thunder and hail, sometimes there is snow. I cannot explain everything, but I know this: try to change things, and you will find the consequences are often different from what you might have expected."

The fox said: "That may be so, but it has been raining a lot recently. And even when it is not raining, the marshes are wet. It is easy to get wet feet. Would it not be good just to have a spell of dry weather?"

Broadhead said: "Dry weather may come soon."

The fox said: "I know how you can change the weather, and I know how you might bring dry weather now."

Broadhead said: "You talk a lot, and you are determined to say what you want to say. I will listen."

The fox said: "You will have heard about the one they call Heave. They say he is a weather god, or a rain man. You will know he lives in the woods in Oakdale. They say that Oakdale is the wettest of all places to live, and all because of this Heave. The clouds follow him wherever he walks, but most of all they gather there in that valley. You will have heard that he has a certain staff. Perhaps it is an oak branch. Perhaps it is a club. It hardly matters how I describe it. I think you understand what I mean. Maybe you have heard that it is this staff that Heave uses to summon storms. He calls his staff Lightness, though if you saw it in action, you would not think it tender or light. If you want to take that staff, I believe I can help you."

Broadhead said: "I have also heard about this staff, but I have no use for it."

The fox said: "I suppose that if this Heave cannot use the staff to bring rain or storms, we will have a weather change, and everything will be better."

Broadhead said: "It does rain a lot. Perhaps if it rained a little less, things would be better."

The fox said: "I cannot take the staff. The Elders would suspect me at once. It is better that you take it yourself. And I don't imagine they would ever guess that it was you who had taken it."

Broadhead said: "How will I get it then?"

The fox said: "You must take it while he is asleep. But be careful. While he is asleep, you may think he looks like a tall oak tree. And his club, Lightness, looks like an oak branch. There are many oak trees in Oakwood, and many oak branches, so it may be difficult to find the right branch, and if you are not quick, he may wake up, and things would be difficult for you then."

Broadhead said: "How will I get it then?"

And so the fox told him how. And the giant did as he had promised, and he let the fox go.

* * *

Heave woke up one day, and he found that his club, Lightness, was gone.

Robin said: "No it was not me who took your club. And I don't suppose you will ever guess who took it."

Some weeks passed, and it didn't rain at all.

Heave said: "Perhaps it was not you who took it, but I have an idea that you know who did it. And if you don't tell me, then things will not go well for you."

Robin said: "Of course I will tell you. Why didn't you ask me this before? I imagine your club was stolen by a giant while you were asleep. That giant's name is Broadhead, and he lives beyond the shores of Broadwater. If you visit him there, I suppose you might find your club."

* * *

So Heave went to the cliff where he knew the giant lived, and he called out: "Broadhead, you have a visitor." He shouted loud enough that the trees shook as though there was a strong wind, and some leaves came fluttering down. The call echoed back off the cliff face, and there seemed to be a shifting in the stones around there.

Before long, the cliff opened, and a giant was standing there.

"Who is this who has come to disturb me," the giant said. "Or what do you want?"

"I am just a stable boy," said Heave, "come to work with your horses. It would be a great honour for me to work for such a famous and well-respected giant as you."

"I have no horses," said the giant. "I am surprised you did not know that, as you seem to know so much about me. But if you want to work, we will have to see what you are able to do. Our stores of firewood are running low. It has been so hot and dry that we hardly need a lot of firewood just now. But firewood is good to have, so if you want to make yourself useful you could go into the forest and gather some wood."

Then the giant went back under the mountain, and Heave went off into the forest. There were many tall trees there. Heave pulled up an oak tree by the roots, and he carried it back to the place where the giant lived. He threw the tree to the ground in front of the cliff, and then he returned to the forest. Before long, he had brought back fifteen trees, and a tangle of trunks and broken branches was piled up in front of the cliff. Then Heave called out again, and the oak trees shifted and shuddered at the sound of it: "Broadhead, here is your firewood."

"So soon," said Broadhead's voice. But when the cliff opened, the giant could hardly see out. "You idiot," said the giant. "Why have you brought so much wood? And why have you put it here? I can't get out of the door. Get this wood cut up and stacked, and get it shifted out of the way."

So Heave did it.

* * *

The next morning, Broadhead said to Heave: "Today, boy, I would like you to clean my halls under the mountain. This is not an easy task. Others have said that it would take them so long to complete it that they would not even begin. But I saw how you worked yesterday, and I have no doubt that you will be able to do this."

Heave had already seen some parts of Broadhead's halls. But there were other parts that he had not seen before. And it seemed that nowhere in those halls had been cleaned for some time.

Heave said: "I will have to go out to find something to clean these halls with."

Outside the sky was clear, and the sun shone. The ground was dry. Parts of that hillside that would usually be damp and marshy were dry. A stream bed that passed by was dry.

A seagull flew through the cloudless skies overhead. Ridge upon ridge of mountains stretched out as far as the sea. And in the distance of the clear day, a hawk watched from where it sat on a hilltop.

Widefaring says: "And did you see them talking, the giant and the stable boy? Did you see the giant ask him to clean the halls?"

Farseer says: "I saw more than you might suppose. Those halls were filthy. But outside, the stream was dry."

Widefaring says: "And did you see him? Did you see what the stable boy did?"

Farseer says: "I saw him climbing the mountain, crossing the grassy ground. I saw him digging near the tarn. I hardly understood it at first, the sun shone, the sky was clear, the tarn was deep and blue, why would he climb the mountain to dig? But yes, I saw it."

Widefaring says: "I flew further than you might have guessed. I was there. I saw him digging. I saw the water flow. I saw the cascade tumbling down the mountainside, the flood waters heading for Broadhead's halls."

Farseer says: "The giant may have had his halls cleaned, but he didn't enjoy it. Things were not going so well for him since he took that club, and he might have wanted to give it back."

Widefaring says: "If Broadhead was suffering with his new stable boy, the rest of the land was suffering as well. Did you see what happened next, or how long the land lasted without rain?"

Farseer says: "I saw the land dry and parched, I saw trees wilting, I saw smoke on the mountains."

Widefaring says: "And did you see them talking, the giant and the stable boy? Did you see them planning the fishing trip?"

Farseer says: "I have seen that giant fishing many times before. I saw them talking, but the lake level was low. I saw drowned buildings emerging from the shrinking waters. Giants built that place, long ago. A secret place, few know about it now. It is difficult to use buildings that lie hidden beneath the surface of a lake."

Widefaring says: "And did you see them out on the water?"

Farseer says: "I saw the two of them in that little boat. I saw the stable boy wrestling with something under the water. I saw how the boat rocked, and how the giant struggled with the new reality. He knew what he had done. But he didn't know who had come to visit him."

Widefaring says: "That giant would love to give back the club."

Two giants sat in the twilight. There in the faraway fells, in the rocks, they watched the sun set behind a ridge. The evening was warm, but those giants were not fond of the sunlight.

Longleg said: "How has it come to this? Did you think about what would happen?"

Broadhead said: "I thought about it more than you assume. The fox told the story about the rain. But what I thought was this: if that Heave does not have his club, he can hardly walk out into our lands and strike us down with it. He can hardly beat us, or crack his club against our bodies. What I thought was that maybe we would have a quieter life. But that has not happened.

"I would gladly return that club if things would go back to the way they were before. But it is dangerous to go walking in Oakdale. I have a stable boy working for me now. I will give him the club and ask him to take it back. He seems to be able to get things done, even if he has an unconventional approach to work."

The skies were clear. A seagull flew overhead. In the distance, a hawk perched on a mountaintop and gazed out as far as it could see.

Widefaring says: "And did you see the giant fetch the club Lightness, from where he had hidden it under the mountain? And did you see him hand it to the one who had lost it, though he hardly knew what he was doing? And did you see Heave raise the club, and swing, and crack? And did you see the giant crumble? And did you see the gathering clouds? I saw all of this, but I don't suppose you saw it."

Farseer says: "I saw more than you could guess. The clouds appeared on the mountaintops, Snowbell, and Anvil, and Skybarrow. And it rained for a long time after that."

Smith in Micklewood

There is a great forest called Micklewood, and in the middle of that forest there is a waterfall called Forest Force. Beside the beck there is a forge, and that forge belongs to a certain Smith.

That forge is a magnificent building. Many fine and precious things have been made there. The sharpest swords, the hardest helmets, jewelled necklaces, and red-gold rings. All these things were made by Smith in his forge. A stream of crystal water from a pool above the waterfall was diverted to run through the middle of the forge for plunging and quenching. And Smith has boys who work the woodland, coppicing willow and hazel, and bringing charcoal for the forge fires.

But it is easy to pass that way without seeing the forge. From the outside the building could be mistaken for a simple wooden cattle shed, turned grey with age. The ringing of the hammers and the clamour of voices in the forge can be drowned out by the roar of the waterfall. But even the beck itself may be hard to find. The sounds of milk-white water churning and splashing against rocks, chattering downstream, may be swallowed by the silence of Micklewood. It is easy to become disorientated in the great forest. The chattering you hear may be the chattering of birds. The rustling may be the rustling of beech leaves in the wind. There may be cracks beneath your feet as fallen branches break. It is easy to become alone and astray in Micklewood, not seeing a path, unsure which way to turn.

* * *

This was a time when the walls of Highgarth had been recently built. And the Elders, who at that time were still newly arrived in the world, were worrying about their place in it.

Fairhair said: "Heave is certainly strong, but if he is to defend us against the giants, he must be stronger. I have seen those giants, how they wander through this land. They seem to know no fear. It is as though they may walk right up to the walls of Highgarth whenever they choose."

And so she left Highgarth and walked into the great forest of Micklewood to find Smith.

You have heard about the workshop of Smith in Micklewood. Smith is known throughout the whole world as a maker of great wonders. He made the hamper Ampleful: food for one man would be put in it, and when it was opened, food for a hundred men would be found in it. He made the chariot Allspeed: if a man got into it, he could wish to be anywhere in the world, wherever he wanted, and he would be there quickly. He made the sword Firebright: it was the sharpest of swords, and no-one could escape the one who held it. These are some of the treasures Smith made, but he made many more.

Smith said to Fairhair: "I don't feel the giants are a great threat. If anyone walked through these woods with bad intentions, or meaning to do us harm, I am not sure they would be able to find us here."

Fairhair said: "It may be that you are safe here, out of sight of those who wish to destroy you. Not all of us are so lucky."

Smith said: "If you are afraid of the giants, I don't know how I can help you."

Fairhair said: "You have made many beautiful things. Now do this for me: make a belt for Heave, so that when he wears it he will be strong enough to defend us from these attacks."

Smith said: "Very well, I can make the belt, and I will be pleased to do it. For it is my greatest joy to make the most beautiful treasures."

Many small dwarfs worked there with Smith, and each one had his own part to play in the making of things. Each one had his own special skill. And anyone who worked with Smith had to be the best at that thing, whatever it might be. Some worked the bellows, some worked the hammers. Some identified and gathered the right rocks that were needed for metal making. Some cut precious stones. Some designed patterns or drew decorations, others carved, others bent metals into wonderful shapes, others added colour, though I cannot say how they did it. Each one was an expert in his own area, and each one was dedicated to maintaining his mastery of his particular speciality. None of those dwarfs really understood what the others were doing, and yet when they all came together, they were able to make the most beautiful treasures.

When the belt was done, Smith said: "Why is the belt so beautiful? The power of this belt is bound up in the patterns that adorn it. These are not mere decorations. The twisting beasts give the belt its strength."

* * *

One of the dwarfs who worked in that place was called Dragonfly. He was an expert in colour. So whenever there was a need to change the colour of a particular material, or where there were patterns to be made in red or blue or another colour, Dragonfly was one of the dwarfs who would be called upon to do that.

Dragonfly didn't work on the belt. He was not involved with the mistake in the pattern, the small flaw that meant that the belt would weaken as time passed. He was not the dwarf who was missing from the forge on the day the belt was to be made, and who had to be replaced. And he was not the dwarf who was called in to help with the belt, to replace the missing dwarf. He was not that dwarf, called in to work on an area that was not quite his own. Dragonfly was not involved in the belt incident at all. But he saw what had happened. He saw the belt before it left the workshop, before Smith handed it to Fairhair to take back to Heave to wear in his defence of Highgarth.

I suppose dwarfs will always think about the future, or what the future might hold, or whether their dreams about the future might ever become real, or what they might have to do to change their own situation, or when it might be time to take action. And I suppose that if something were to happen that could cause a dwarf to pause, or to reassess how he was spending his days, then that might be a moment when the dwarf might decide to take action, or to make a change that could affect his future.

Surrounded by talent, busy, working in a well-equipped work-shop, it is easy to think great thoughts, or it is easy for a dwarf's mind to wander into dreams of what might be. It is easy to imagine that similar opportunities could also exist in other places. Or it is easy to forget the reasons why a dwarf might have left everything behind in the first place to come to the famous smithy in Micklewood. After all, dwarfs do come and go from that place, from time to time.

So when Dragonfly saw what happened with the belt, he did make up his mind to make a change. "Maybe it is time to go back home," he said.

* * *

And so Dragonfly left the forge for the final time. He faced the north, and he started walking. Micklewood is a great forest, and it is not easy to cross from one side to the other, or to come to the edge from the middle. But when Dragonfly reached the edge of that forest, the longest and most difficult part of his journey was still ahead of him. He came out of the trees onto rough open land, and his next obstacle came clearly into view. High mountains rose up directly in front of him, blocking the way northwards, their grim grey faces paying no heed to the small dwarf looking up at them.

But Dragonfly was filled with hope about things to come. He was thinking about the new life he would build for himself back home in the north. He was thinking about how things would be better than what he had left behind in Micklewood. And driven by these thoughts, he set off merrily through the difficult and unfamiliar landscape.

He pressed ahead to the lower slopes, stony and suddenly steep. Rocky outcrops appeared, and cliffs and boulders, with shadows where anything might hide. "The hills are wild, and bigger than I could imagine," Dragonfly said. "But there are ways through these lands. Dwarfs have walked these ways before."

> High above the barren valley
> A landmark seen on a lofty top
> Dark figures on the skyline
> Two beasts turned to stone
> A moment frozen in time

Were they held together in peace?
Or in a wild attack?
Friends or enemies held close
A last moment to last for ever

*

A pile of stones at a high pass
Barren wind-bitten place
A monument was raised
A memorial for a forgotten hero
An unremembered god or king

*

It's hard to walk on the high ridge
Better in the valley bottom
Shadows grow and thickets spread
Briar and bramble coil and grasp
In the sheltered valley

*

A long lake in the valley bottom
Whipped by a bitter wind
Trees on the island drenched by spray
A small shelter, a hut half hidden
How can anyone live there?

The dwarf hurried on past all these places. He started to recognise parts of the landscape long unseen, and he knew that soon he would be back home.

And then there was the fell Anvil up ahead. And there was the wide valley, rough open land filled with marshes and scattered groups of trees. Dragonfly entered a patch of woodland, hardly big enough to be called a wood. Birches gave a yellow green hue to the light that passed between their leaves, and their silver trunks brightened the woodland floor. But from anywhere in those woods, the edge of the trees could clearly be seen. This was not Micklewood. Was it smaller than he had remembered? Was everything smaller?

* * *

Toadstool said: "Why did you leave? Most people know that Smith in Micklewood is the greatest smith and the greatest maker. I suppose most people would consider it an honour to work in the workshop there. Few would choose to leave if they had the honour of working in that workshop."

Dragonfly said: "I suppose I must have had good reasons for doing it, or otherwise I would not have left."

Toadstool said: "Things that have not been explained may be hard to understand. It is easy to take a wrong turn when descending in the mist. If it was me, I don't believe I would have left. Or if I were to get a position to work with Smith in Micklewood, I don't believe I would then leave."

Dragonfly said: "It is easy for you to say that, but you hardly know what you would do. You hardly know whether you would have chosen to leave unless you were there."

Toadstool said: "It is easy to take a wrong turn. Smith in Micklewood is a great smith with a great workshop. Many want to work there, and if I had the chance to work there I would not leave."

Cobweb said: "You must be happy to be back."

Dragonfly said: "I can say this: it is very different to be back. Life here is very different from life in Micklewood, but also things are very different here from how I remember them. If there were things that I was unhappy with in Micklewood, then I am happy to have left those things behind. It is also true that there were things from here that I missed while I was away. I was many years in Micklewood, and all that time I missed this place. And now I am back, but things are not how they were before. Things that are past and gone may never return. I have come back to a place, but I have not come back to a time. If there were things from here that I missed when I was away, there are still things from here that I miss now that I am back. I can say this: very little here is as I remember it."

Cobweb said: "Or do you miss Micklewood then?"

Dragonfly said: "Of course there are things I miss in Micklewood. Life was not so terrible there. If it was so terrible, I would not have stayed there for as long as I did. And yet there were also things I didn't like, and I am glad to have left those things behind."

Toadstool said: "The great workshop, the joy of creating such beauty, the joy of working together, the songs!"

Dragonfly said: "Of course there are things I miss. And there are things I am happy to have left behind."

Toadstool said: "Why would you come here to this place?"

Dragonfly said: "When I was here before, before I went to Micklewood, there were many paths I could have chosen to follow. A great opportunity opened up for me to go to Micklewood, and I took it. But that was not the only way I could have chosen. What better place to return to now, to find new opportunities."

Toadstool said: "Surely there are better places to be."

Dragonfly said: "I can believe there may be better places, but I don't know where those places are. Better to be in a place I know well, knowing its upsides and downsides. An unknown place will always bring new surprises. There should be few surprises for me here, anything I make I will make myself."

Toadstool said: "And was Smith pleased when you left his workshop, or what did he think? I hardly think anyone who has seen the inside of Smith's workshop would be allowed to work elsewhere again."

Dragonfly said: "There are stories, I know, of dwarfs who have disappeared, whether they drowned in the white waters of Forge Force, or whether they were lost in the woods. But as you can see, I am here."

Cobweb said: "And what will you work on now, or what did you work on in Micklewood?"

Dragonfly said: "I mainly worked on colour, on getting the colour right in the fine fragments that are used to put together patterns."

Cobweb said: "Oh. But they say you are very skilled. I suppose you could also make other things."

Dragonfly said: "Well yes, I could make other things in the same way, other precious fragments."

Cobweb said: "And will you do that then? Make fragments? Or will you make bigger things? Whole things?"

Dragonfly said: "The truth is, I cannot work here in the same way that I worked in Micklewood. There are two reasons. The first is: I have the skills and the knowledge to do that work, but here in these small woods in the north I don't have the tools to do it. And neither can I get those tools. The tools I would need are very rare and precious, and they are only found in Smith's workshop. The second reason is: it is difficult to work on such things alone. In the forge in Micklewood each one of us played a small part in a bigger team, or each one of us worked on a small part of what was then put together to make the finished piece."

Toadstool said: "It is easy to replace one lost part of such a machine. It is more difficult for the lost part to replace the whole of the rest of the machine."

Greystone said: "Even a rough or shapeless thing can be carved into something precious. Chip away the crust from the surface to reveal beauty beneath."

Beeswing said: "There is often power in fragile beauty. Do not mistake lightness for weakness. Appearances may be deceptive."

Dewdrop said: "How bright we shine, and then soon we are gone."

Memory said: "Telling and retelling, memories of memories last longer in our minds."

Cobweb said: "There are so many things you could do in the future."

Toadstool said: "I don't believe I would have left Micklewood."

The Discovery of Music

The girl crouched on the mountaintop and shivered. The wind was blowing, and it was very exposed. The ground fell away steeply on all sides, and there was nothing to see but mist and empty air. She was hardly dressed for mountain climbing. The cloak she wore was pulled tight around her body and over her head, and when it slipped, her bare arms and legs were exposed to the cold. Wisps of hair that had been tied back had come free, and now blew around her red cheeks and into her eyes. You may think she was crouching to try to keep sheltered from the wind. But there was another reason.

Many people had told her that a certain bird could be found on that mountaintop, sitting and watching. She had climbed that mountain to speak to that bird, and the bird was there, just as she had hoped. Now she was crouching down so that she might hear what it had to say.

Farseer said: "I saw Skyrunner as he wandered from place to place. I saw him knocking on many doors. That lasted a long time. But I have not seen Skyrunner for some time now.

"I remember Skyrunner's song. I heard that song, and I suppose you may remember hearing it as well. Skyrunner was a great singer. No-one can doubt it. I have not heard a better singer. Without that song there would be nothing here around us, only emptiness. There would be nothing to see.

"And yet I know that that is not what you are looking for.

"When Skyrunner sang, those words were not his own. He had heard those songs many times before. He had learned them from other, older voices. I know he spent a long time learning those songs, practicing his art, rehearsing for his masterpiece performance. I saw in his face how happy he was with how he sang.

"But you are looking for something else.

"Skyrunner sang about music. I remember it. He sang about new things and transformation. He sang about constancy and eternal truth. He sang about the sound of thought. I know well what Skyrunner sang. I know what you are looking for, and where you might find it. Listen carefully and I will tell you."

The girl didn't speak. She tried to stop her teeth from chattering. She tried to stay still and concentrate on the bird's words, though her legs were growing numb and the wind had found new ways under her cloak. When she nodded her head the cloak fell back a little more, but she didn't move. She listened to what the bird said.

Farseer said: "I know of three waterfalls, loud and fast-flowing. Each one is in a faraway corner of the land. Each one is guarded by a certain spirit, a water elf. I have seen those elves many times, always singing, or playing music on a harp. The first is in the south in Greywood. The falls at Smith's forge are well known. That water has hardened many swords. The second is in the north at Blackwater. The water falls from the moorland to the lake in a single drop. The third is in the west in Deepdale. The waterfall is seldom seen, almost hidden in a deep ravine.

"Now I have told you where you must go to find what you are looking for. You will find three women in those places. They will have something to say to you, though it may not be what you want to hear. This is how you might achieve a full mastery of music. This is what you asked me about, and now I have told you what you wanted to know."

Then the bird stopped talking. It seemed to be watching something far in the distance.

The girl didn't stay on the mountain top long, she hurried down to the sheltered valley below.

* * *

There were two sisters who lived by a long lake. Their father was there. He could hardly walk as he was so old, and he could hardly see. There were many ducks on that lake, and the two sisters looked after the ducks, and they looked after their father.

One sister said to the other sister: "I will not stay here for ever. I will go out and learn something in the world." That girl was called Hope, and you have heard, she climbed the mountain to speak with the hawk who she found sitting there.

The other sister was called Constance, and she said: "I will stay here. I am satisfied with what I have here, or who knows what I will find closer to home?"

* * *

Hope had seen the forest laid out in front of her as she came down from the mountain. From far away she had seen it, the whole forest blanketing the landscape. Beneath the trees, there were long valleys separated by low-lying spurs, bounded by long lakes that reached out from the mountains towards the sea. But now she reached the edge of the vastness of that forest, trees rose up above her and ahead of her, and bushy growth blocked the view of where she might walk. She could see only a hundred yards or so ahead, or where the woods were thicker she could see much less. In the fell landscapes around the high mountains, it is easy to see the shape of the land. Or it is easy to see a peak for orientation, or easy to follow a ridge or a valley. Under the trees, things were quite different.

The girl walked for a long time in that forest. Sometimes when her way was blocked by a cliff or a stream or a thicket or a fallen tree, she had to make her way around the obstruction, and then it was difficult for her to be sure which direction she had been walking in. One group of trees may look much like another, and often she thought she might be passing by a place where she had already walked. Sometimes she tried to follow a stream, but streams meander, and sometimes they run into thick vegetation. It is easy for a stream to pass through a thicket, but it is more difficult for a girl. Sometimes she walked into the night, though it was not always easy to see in the darkness under the trees.

One time, she was walking at night, and she came to a clearing. And when she looked up, she could see what had been hidden from her by the trees. It was the Winter Road in the sky, showing her the way she should walk. And when she walked that way, she reached a place where the water fell white. She heard music in the waterfall, and she could walk no further, but she lay down by the side of the stream, and she slept. And while she slept, she dreamed a dream. She dreamed of the place that she had found in the forest, the trees, the waterfall. And in her dream, there was an elf-woman there, singing to the stars.

When she awoke, she saw that it was not only a dream, for there was a woman there, sitting beside her. The woman was dressed in green, but her hair was white.

Hope said to the woman: "Are you an elf?"

The elf said: "There are many things you might have chosen to say when you woke up. But you chose this."

Hope said: "I have come a long way for your sake, and wandered for a long time in this forest. It is strange that this place is called Forge Force when there is no sign of any forge. It might just as well be called Forest Force, and few could say that that would be a bad name."

The elf woman spoke with a musical tone. She said: "I don't suppose you would have had an easier time finding your way here if the waterfall had been called by any other name. But if you have wandered through these woods for such a long time to find me here, tell me: why have you come, or what did you want from me?"

Hope said: "I want to sing. I have come here to learn how to sing the songs I have in my mind."

The elf said: "I can teach you this: listen and learn. But most of all, do."

Hope stayed there with the elf woman for some time, but then she set off again on her journey.

* * *

A place that is hidden in the depths of the woods may be hard to find. Sometimes it may even seem difficult to find a way out of a forest. But this is not an impossible task. Persistence is a path that leads out of the forest. This path leads to the edge of the trees and the dark expanse can be left behind.

There is a waterfall in the north. This is what Hope had been told. So once she had come out of the great forest, she set off northwards, and she climbed up into the mountains again.

The days passed, and she found herself on a smooth, grassy ridge that stretched away into the distance. It is often easy to make progress along a mountain ridge. Sometimes she walked and sometimes she ran. She passed over rounded summits marked by piles of stones, and still the ridge stretched out before her. Golden sheep grazed there, and small birds called high overhead. Far below her, to her right and to her left, long lakes lay in the valleys that ran parallel to the way she was walking. There was no shelter anywhere on that smooth ridge. But as long as she was up there, the wind did not blow, so it was pleasant enough.

Hope came to the top of a grassy hill. There was a pile of stones there, and sitting beside those stones she saw two dwarfs.

Hope said to the dwarfs: "I am looking for a waterfall, I have heard it is somewhere in this part of the country."

Roseleaf said: "That waterfall is called High Force, and I know where you might find it."

Goldenstone said: "It is a sacred place, the elf woman is always there, and she is always singing."

Roseleaf said: "It is not far from here. The waterfall is in the trees below this ridge, and the water falls from a high valley down to the shore of the lake."

Goldenstone said: "It is a sad song, and she sings to the stars because they are old, and they remember everything that was here and that is now lost. And they love to hear this sad song sung."

Roseleaf said: "It is a beautiful song."

Goldenstone said: "She is always singing."

Hope saw the trees far below her, she left the ridge, and she made her way down to the beck that flowed loudly down its rocky path. She weaved her way down through the tall trees, past the fern and moss and wet rock, to the pool at the bottom of the waterfall, where the thundering waters grew suddenly calm. Hope could hear the music in the sound of the waterfall, the rumble and the roar below, and a sparkle of melody. And she could hear a woman's voice, singing.

She stopped to listen. It was as though she had heard the songs before, and yet she didn't know them. The songs were familiar, and yet also unfamiliar.

And then Hope saw the woman who was singing. She was sitting beside the pool at the bottom of the waterfall. She was all in green and brown, and it was hard to see her at first in the soft light that had made its way down through the trees. She was the size of an ordinary woman, but she seemed small in that setting, among the huge trees, the high waterfall, the great rocks.

Hope said to the woman: "I have come a long way for your sake, and I believe you can teach me something."

The elf said: "Tell me this then, who are you, or why have you come here?"

Hope said: "I came here to this waterfall to find an elf woman, and I believe I have found her."

The elf said: "Tell me this then if you have come so far: what is it you want to learn?"

Hope said: "There are songs I want to sing, but they are not songs I have heard before. They are only in my mind."

The elf said: "I can teach you this: if you want to write your own song, you can do this. If you want to sing a song, you should feel it. Write it so that you feel it when you sing it."

Hope stayed there with the elf woman for some time, and then she set off again on her journey.

* * *

There is a waterfall in the west. This is what Hope had been told. So she set off westwards, and after a while she found a way that led along the bottom of a wide valley towards the sea.

This was an old road. It was one of the old roads that the Elders had found when they came into the land. Already built, much trodden, long left to lie. They called these the giants' roads. And this road was called Wade's road. And they told the story of how the giant Wade walked out of the sea in the north, and how he led his cattle along this road, through the heart of the land, through a gap in the mountains, along long valleys, sometimes turning, sometimes stretching straight, all the way to the southern shore to the sea again.

Wade's road was a well-built road, and easier to walk on than much of the surrounding rough country, so this was the way Hope took as she walked out of the high mountains towards the sea.

As the land flattened out, the giant's road swung northwards, so Hope left this road behind, and she headed for the seashore. South she walked along the coast. Seagulls flew there, mewing and circling. Sometimes she passed desolate boats laid on the shingle, old and deserted. And after some days, she saw an old man sitting in a chair by the seashore. He was gazing out to sea.

Hope said to the old man: "I am looking for a waterfall, I have heard it is somewhere in this part of the country."

The old man said: "Many people passing by here ask me the way to where they might want to go. It is often easy for them to persuade me to tell them what I know."

And so the girl gave him a coin.

The old man said: "I know of a waterfall called Fairy Force. It is not far from here. If you follow this valley inland you will find it. Walk towards the highest peaks you will see, but stay in the valley bottom. If you follow this river upstream, and walk for the rest of today, you will find the waterfall."

So she left the sea behind, and she walked inland. She made her way along the valley bottom with the highest peaks ahead of her. She followed alongside the river. And soon she had reached the waterfall. The water had carved out a deep ravine in the fellside. Tall trees filled this cleft, growing all the way up the steep slopes to the sunnier upper reaches. At the foot of the waterfall was a dark pool, where the white water all at once grew calm and still. And mossy rocks and pebbles were lit by dappled green light shining through the trees.

Almost at once, she heard music in the sound of the water. But when she stopped to listen, it seemed to change. She heard the notes of an instrument, sometimes short and quick, dancing and disappearing, but sometimes long and glorious. And then it was a song she heard in the water, a singer strong and true, but she couldn't recognise the words.

And behind the waterfall there was a woman. It was difficult to tell her age. Her hair was not grey like an old woman, but neither was it blonde or dark. Her hair was the colour of roses. She was like no woman the girl had ever seen before. And though the place was

139

guarded by the curtain of falling water, the place itself was dry, so that two cats who hate to wet their fur played happily on the rocky floor.

Hope said to the woman: "Are you an elf?"

The elf said: "I should ask you who you are, for I often sit here but I have never seen you come this way before."

Hope said: "The truth is this: I came this way because I was hoping to find an elf woman who could help me. I have heard that she sits and sings by the waterfall. If it is you that I am looking for, I have come a long way for your sake."

The elf said: "If you have found me by the waterfall, why were you looking, or what did you want to know?"

Hope said: "I have spoken to your sisters at Forge Force and High Force, and I came this way because I hoped you could teach me something."

The elf said: "I can see you have come a long way. Tell me then, what is it you want to ask me?"

Hope said: "There are songs I want to sing. There are things I want to say in music. I came here to learn how to sing these songs."

The elf said: "I can teach you this: the song is music. The words may be hidden, which is to say, people may love the sound of the sung words before they even hear the meaning of the words. This gives power."

Then the elf said: "Joy, sadness, and lullaby: these are the things you have learned, but they were already within you. Now you have heard all that we have to say. You may be frustrated at the outcome of this journey. The power you seek is nothing any of us can teach you. You have it within you. It is part of you. Sing what is in your heart. Play the notes to reflect your own will. Paint the music that is in your mind. That is creation. We cannot teach you how to do it. Sing a new song."

Then the elf said: "When they hear the songs you sing, many men will want to come and find you. They will walk for miles to find you, wherever you are. Some would have come even if you had not made this journey to see us. Others may choose not to come. Others may be far away on their own quests. But many will come."

Hope said: "My sister sits at home. How then will songs be written about her, or how will any such songs be sung?"

The elf said: "There is a song already written about your sister. It will be sung for many years. A certain hero overcame many dangers and passed many trials to reach that girl. It is only right that there should be a song in her honour."

Hope said: "But who wrote that song, or who will sing it?"

The elf said: "A hero passed through fire and water for her. He tamed the beasts, he overcame the gatekeeper, and he won the maiden. He didn't write that song himself. You may think the song is about that hero. But without your sister, the song lacks any purpose, any meaning, or any heart. With a song this great, she may be happy even if there are no more songs."

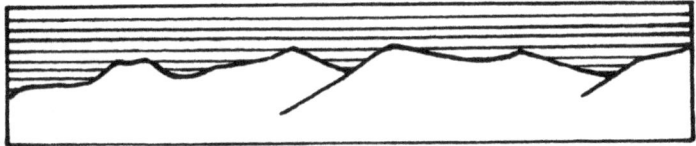

So Hope left that waterfall behind, and she returned home. When she got to the house, her sister came out to meet her, but things were not as they had been.

Hope said: "Why are you dressed like this, with your hair up, like a married woman, or who are these children holding onto your skirts?"

Constance said: "Yes, while you were away, I did get married, and these three boys are my children."

Hope said: "Tell me then, how did it happen?"

Constance said: "Many men came here. They had heard tell of the two sisters who lived between the freshwater and the sea, though when they came I was the only one who was here. It was only the best of them that managed to pass the traps and snares to reach me. We were married not long after that. And these boys will become great singers or musicians, and I will teach them."

Hope said: "How will you teach them?"

Constance said: "I will teach them what I already know about music, with all that is in my own heart."

And so it was. One girl discovered all there was to know about music. And her sister's three sons also all grew up to be fine musicians and singers themselves.

* * *

Hope says: "Do you know the secret places where the elf women in the waterfalls sing to the stars?"

Constance says: "Discovery is when you find things you did not already know."

The Loss of the Luck, part I

Many of the old stories are set in the ancient woodlands, which are also called the great forests. And of all of these forests, Micklewood is the greatest.

A robin flew in the woods. There was a crow there. The robin spoke to the crow, and the crow listened to all the robin had to say. And small birds chattered in the treetops. A seagull flew overhead, long wandering, far flying, far from the sea. And in the distance a hawk saw it all. And anyone who listened to what the birds were saying would know what was coming, provided they could understand the language of birds.

An old man walked alone along the lake shore. He had walked that way when he was younger, but now he was old and grey. He heard the chattering of the small birds, and he knew what was to come.

* * *

One of the Elders was called Wonder. His wife was called Ranwen. Ranwen was tall and strong with long black hair. She knew a lot about what was happening in the world, or which of the Elders was doing what, because she made it her business to know these things. She often put on her black walking cloak and walked through the land to visit the Elders where they lived in their halls in the valleys away from Highgarth. And the Elders were happy to see her come, and they were happy to talk to her, because she was considered very wise. You may have heard these things about Ranwen. But you may not have heard so much about Wonder, as he had done very little of note.

Ranwen was not satisfied with her husband, Wonder. "Why do you always sit around?" she said. "Other men are out in the world doing great deeds, but I see you here every day. Do you not dream of improving your position? Or are you happy to be so badly thought of?"

Wonder thought about what his wife said to him. But he was happy to live a quiet life. In fact, he thought less about about how he might become more spectacular, or how he might achieve greatness, and more about how he might be more satisfied if his life was even quieter, and he was even calmer.

* * *

One time, Ranwen sat in her room and sewed. She was stitching dark patterns on dark-dyed cloth. She was thinking about her husband, she was thinking about the world, and she was thinking about the pattern she was sewing. She thought about how she had designed that pattern of black leaves and black flowers, bound together by twisting and coiling stems, and she thought about how she might change it in one way or another, or how she might make it better.

And as she sewed, a dragonfly flew in through the open window. That dragonfly was a curious thing. It shone like a jewel. For a moment it shone red like garnet, and then it was like bluestone, and then yellow as buttercups. The glittering dragonfly landed on Ranwen's lap where she was holding her stitching, and it began to speak.

And the dragonfly said to Ranwen: "You have walked in the world, and you have learned many things, but how do you plan to use all the knowledge you have gathered?"

And Ranwen said: "I have not thought about that. I thought only that learning was a good thing in itself."

And the dragonfly said: "Mindrace is hardly ever here at High-garth – where does he spend all his time? He clings to his position of power like an old man afraid of retirement. He clearly sees that he has become irrelevant. He uses all his skill to preserve his own position, and does no real good for those he claims to lead. Many people have seen this, though few dare speak it."

Ranwen said: "It is strange that a dragonfly should fly into my room and start to talk to me. And what a strange speech from such a small creature! I have never heard anything like this said before."

And the dragonfly said: "Many big things grow from small beginnings."

And Ranwen said: "Those who are too small to get what they want on their own must find someone else to get it for them."

The dragonfly said: "The minds of even the smallest creatures are big enough to hold greatness. Anyone can have a big idea. Thoughts are given freely. You heard these things first from me, but the thoughts are now your own."

And then the dragonfly leapt into the air. It fluttered, it hovered, and it was away. And it sparkled as it flew, with many colours reflecting the sunlight.

* * *

Ranwen thought about what had happened, and she thought about what it might mean. Later, she went to speak to her husband.

Ranwen said: "Mindrace wanders wide in the world. Perhaps it is time for someone else to sit in the high seat, so often left unoccupied. It is a bad ruler who leaves the seat of power empty."

Wonder said: "Why are you telling me this? Things are not so bad, and they could be worse. Or who do you think would want to take Mindrace's place as leader?"

Ranwen said: "You should sit in the empty seat. Many would be glad to see you there."

Wonder said: "It is unwise to act against a lucky man. And Mindrace is lucky."

Ranwen said: "Mindrace's luck will fail. Everyone knows his luck is bound up in a certain stone. And if he was to lose that stone, or to leave it behind, someone else could take it. He would not be so lucky then."

Wonder said: "I find it hard to believe that Mindrace would leave that stone behind."

Ranwen said: "You may believe what you want. But I already have it. I took that stone from him myself. It hardly matters now whether he knows it or not. I have the stone here, and now I give it to you."

Wonder said: "This cannot be the Luck. It is an ordinary enough stone that could have come from any stream."

Ranwen said: "It is the Luck. It may look ordinary, but it has brought him great power. And now it will bring the same power to you."

And so Wonder took the stone from her, and he held it in his hand. Perhaps he thought that by going along with his wife's wishes he really would be happier. Perhaps he was curious to see whether his life really could change for the better, or to see what would happen if he held the Luck. Would his luck suddenly change? Had luck somehow been eluding him until now? There was only one way to find out.

* * *

Wonder called all the Elders to a meeting in the high hall at Highgarth, and he said: "Mindrace wanders wide. How is it that we never see our leader? Would it not be better to have a leader who was actually here with us?"

There were murmurs among the assembled Elders.

"It is true that Mindrace is hardly here. But things are not so bad. Why change?"

"Who could lead us? Heave is our strength, the one who is our strength protects us, and he could lead us. Simmering is our cook, he feeds us, and he could lead us. Smith creates many things, and he could lead us. But these people already have their own roles. What would happen if things were to change?"

"Giants have been seen in Micklewood. What business does Smith have with those giants? It is hardly surprising that they should seek him out."

"Mindrace has been lucky, but we all know his luck is bound up in a certain stone. How would it be if he somehow lost that stone, or if someone else found it?"

"Maybe Mindrace's luck has run out."

Then Wonder spoke again: "I can lead. I will use my position of power to keep things as they are, or to let things remain the same. I hardly want to see everything changed. We are well enough. A change here could cause unknown or unintended consequences for all of us. Change for its own sake is not a sensible objective. From now on, things will be just as they were before."

And then he sat down in the high seat, and he was the leader of the Elders. Wonder enjoyed this position while it lasted. And while it lasted, he felt very lucky.

No-one thought to tell Mindrace about what had happened. But that was partly because no-one knew where Mindrace was.

The Loss of the Luck, part II

Early one morning, the sun was shining, and Mindrace was walking along the shore of a long lake. Golden headed daffodils turned their faces towards him, and above him in the branches of trees, fresh with spring green leaves, the birds were singing.

Mindrace listened to what the birds sang. He could understand the language of birds, but what they said was troubling, and he hardly believed it could be true.

"There goes Mindrace. Once he was called the highest of the high. Now it seems his luck has run out."

"He is far from home now, but so many things have changed there. He may not recognise Highgarth when he returns."

"Who is it who sits in the high seat? Who wears a grey coat in the hall?"

"Who is that? He answers when men call Mindrace's name, but that is not who I call Mindrace."

"I recognise Mindrace. I see an old man in the wilderness far from home. Maybe it is better for him to stay away. He will not like what he sees if he returns to his old hall."

* * *

Mindrace wandered through the world, and a long time passed. But Mindrace had always wandered. Did it make a difference that he was now homeless, or in exile? Many stories are told about Mindrace. But did those things happen while he was in exile or not? It is not always easy to say.

* * *

It was many years later when Mindrace did finally return to Highgarth, but when that happened, everything else quickly followed. It turned out that it didn't really matter whether it was Wonder or Mindrace who held the stone they call Mindrace's luck. It turned out that the Luck belonged to Mindrace all along. There was no great resistance, and there was no great debate. Mindrace was soon seated in the high seat again.

Wonder fled to the east. He passed beyond the end of the world, and into a land that is so hard to describe that some people say it doesn't exist at all. Some say he was soon killed by the giants who live in that place. Others say that he lived for a long time among them there. Ranwen also fled, but she didn't go with her husband. She hid closer to home in one of the great forests. Her dark shape moved between the trees like a shadow. She stayed there in hiding for a long time after that.

The Young Warrior

There was once a young boy. He couldn't find the answers to his questions at home, so he left that place behind him, and he set out into the world to try to find the answers elsewhere. A long path ran along the sea front. By the side of the path there stood a pole, and on top of the pole there sat a bird.

And the boy said to the bird: "Have you heard about that warrior? Tell me: what happened to him, or where is he now?"

And the bird said: "You have not told me the warrior's name, but I can tell you what I know. I heard he was trying to recapture his past glories. I heard he thought he would be able to relive his old life again. He remembered the words of the old songs, praising his great deeds, but the world around him had changed. It is often hard to find a new purpose when the old routines, old goals, old reasons for living are all taken away. I heard he was trying to escape the world, and to send his mind back to what he remembered, back to a time that is past and gone. Mead and wine help a mind remember, and they help it forget."

And the boy said to the bird: "Tell me then: have you heard about the bowl?"

And the bird said: "You have not told me the name of the bowl, but I can tell you what I know. I heard the bowl was broken into pieces. Once it was filled with love. Then it was filled with drink. Then it fell, carelessly dropped, and it lay shattered on the floor."

And the boy said to the bird: "And have you heard about the woman? The warrior's wife, the child's mother."

And the bird said: "I have heard about her. It is hard for me to tell this. She didn't know what to do, or where to go. She fell in love with a broken man. She helped him mend, she gave him what she had. But later, once he recovered, she found that he was not what she had imagined. He has gone. And now her child has gone, looking for his father.

And the boy said to the bird: "Tell me then: have you heard about the child?"

And the bird said: "I have heard about that boy. He longs to be a great warrior like his father. He is searching for the truth about his father, or he is searching for the stories people tell about him or the songs they sing. He has left his mother behind. He is searching for adventure, and he believes that is what he will find.

And the boy thanked the bird, and he continued on his way.

The Woman on the Island

I know of a lake called Blackwater. The lake is long and narrow, and the water is very dark. The wind often blows hard along that valley and whips up waves on the lake. There is an island there called Lingholm, and there is a woman on that island.

She says:

Things that are never joined together
Are easier to break apart

My child is gone, following his father
Searching for one who would not be found

Every day I watch the water
Spending time crying in the rain

Anyone who passes this place:
Can they see beneath the surface?
Can they see the sorrow inside me?

One man, preferring past glories
Memories or imaginings in his mind
Chose to run from change

I was left to walk in exile
Through the tall oaks
Through the briar and bramble

How I miss our time together
Now I spend my life alone
Waiting for news that doesn't come

Dark hills rise over this shady valley
A cruel wind blows on the water
I am on an island

I know of another lake called Broadwater. To the north of that lake there are more trolls, to the west lies a plain that stretches to the sea. I know of another lake called Olderwater. In that lake there are seven islands: Beeholm, Lilyholm, Maidenholm, Silverholm, Lingholm, Henholm, and Birchholm. I know of another lake called Overwater in Oakdale, and there are two islands there.

There are more lakes and more islands.

Ashleaf's Pride

I know of a certain stone. You have probably heard of it. You probably know this stone as Ashleaf's pride. That name comes from Ashleaf, who owned the stone for a time. Before that, it had another name.

There was once a young man called Ashleaf, and he lived in Hawksdale near Marradale. I cannot tell you when it happened that Ashleaf first heard about the stone Winedeep. In those days, everyone knew about that stone, and sometimes people would talk about it. But I will tell you about the time when Ashleaf decided that he must have the stone, and I will tell you about how he went about trying to get it.

One day, Ashleaf was out with some other boys, and those boys were showing each other some of the stones they had found. Because sometimes, when you are out walking, you may see a certain stone on the path, standing out, shining and different from everything around it, and you might stop and pick it up. Some of the boys had pieces of bright white quartz, some had yellow-grey flint. One of the stones was flecked with bright blue-green, another had a dark metallic shine.

All at once, a red-haired man came walking. He saw what the boys were doing, and he said: "You may think these stones are pretty enough, but if you go out further into the world, or away from this valley, you will soon see things that may change your minds."

Ashleaf said: "It may be that there are great wonders far away. But what can you show us? Or is there anything that you have brought back with you from the places you say you've seen?"

The man said: "I have been to many places and seen many things. I have owned many beautiful stones, and I have also sold many. I have held still more in my hands that I could never afford to own. Now I carry the memories in my mind of what I have owned and sold, and of what I have held and given away. The most beautiful stone I remember is called Winedeep. And though I can see it clearly in my own mind, I cannot show it to you."

Ashleaf said: "Many people talk about the stone Winedeep, but fewer can say that they have seen it. You say that you have seen many things, but you have shown us little."

The man said: "I have seen the stone, with my own eyes."

Ashleaf said: "Who has the stone, or where did you see it?"

The man said: "A dwarf has the stone. That dwarf's name is Oldrich, but he is not easy to find."

Ashleaf said: "How can I find the dwarf Oldrich?"

The man said: "I cannot say where that dwarf is now. But I can say this: if you find the dwarf and you see the stone, you will surely want to own it. And that will not be easy for you to do."

Then the man went on his way, and Ashleaf and the other boys were left with their stones.

But Ashleaf did not forget the man's words. He started to think about the beautiful stones that must be so much easier to find far away from Hawksdale. And most of all, he started to think about the stone Winedeep, and how he might find it.

And that was how Ashleaf came to set out on his journey to find the dwarf and to find the stone. I will not tell you about everything that happened along the way, but there are one or two things that are too important to miss.

* * *

There was an old man who lived under a rock in the deep forest. That forest is called Ringwood. It was not easy to find that man. Ashleaf had been into Marradale to ask about the stone. Many people there had no interest in that stone, or many had laughed.

"Why are you asking about such stories?"

"Do you not have work to be doing?"

"These are children's stories. Is it not time for you to forget about these things?"

"There is a bird who knows about these stories. You should ask that bird."

"Magic stones and talking birds, time for you to head back to Hawksdale."

But Ashleaf did find the bird, and the bird told him about the man in Ringwood who lived under a stone. And although it was not easy to find that man, after some time, Ashleaf did find him.

The man said: "If you are interested in stones, then you have come to the right place. I own some of the rarest stones, and I have seen more. I can show you now what I have here. I have seen many other beautiful stones. I have sold many myself, and bought more. I have never seen that stone, though I have heard about it. I didn't know you were looking for that dwarf. Yes, I have met him. He is often at the dwarf market, buying and selling, but I couldn't tell you how you might find that market."

And so Ashleaf left the man, and he went on his way.

* * *

I will not tell everything about how Ashleaf got the gold. It did take time. Many hard days were spent walking from place to place in all weathers. For sometimes the sun does beat down (it can be easy to forget it). There are different stories about how he got the gold, and I cannot say which story is true, or which one I should tell. Some say that he got that gold in a fair way, buying stones cheaply, and selling them to those who would pay more for them. Some say that he won that gold fairly in a bet. Others say that he worked hard for a long time in paid employment until he had earned that gold fairly. Whichever story is true, when Ashleaf finally walked into the dwarf market, he was older, better dressed, and a lot richer.

* * *

And Ashleaf did find the dwarf market, and the dwarf Oldrich was there. And the dwarf did have the stone, and Ashleaf did have the gold he needed to buy it. And so Ashleaf gave the gold to the dwarf, and he took the stone Winedeep, and he held it in his hand.

But at that moment, Ashleaf was seized by an overpowering sense of emptiness. It could not be failure that he was feeling, for did he not now have in his hands the thing he had yearned for for so long? How could fulfilment feel so desolate? Or was it a fear of what might come next, now that he was freed from his long quest. The stone lay in his hand. It had a weight to it. It felt very real.

"It's not what I wanted," he said. "I thought it was what I wanted, but I want to go back. I want things to be the way they were before I got it."

Oldrich said: "It is always difficult to return to how things were before."

Ashleaf said: "Are you not one of those supernaturals? I suppose the supernaturals have the power to travel through time, to go back, just a few steps, just a few moments."

Oldrich said: "It is true, I do have that power."

Ashleaf said: "Take me back then, only by a few moments."

Oldrich said: "Have you forgotten? It was I who made the sale. I have taken your money, and I was pleased to do it. No returns."

Ashleaf said: "I need to go back. I can remember it, just a few moments ago, I still had the choice, I still had the money in my hand. I could have walked away."

Oldrich said: "You have the stone now. There is little point in wishing things were different. You have it, and now it would be better for you to work out how to use it, to move forward, to make it work for you. There is little point in thinking about returning to the past. Everything that was there is past and gone."

Ashleaf said: "But you can go back in time. I know you are one of those supernaturals, and everyone has heard that they have that power."

Oldrich said: "There is little point in thinking these thoughts. Do you think that if you put yourself in exactly the same position again you would react differently? How would it be if I told you that I had taken you back, and we are here now because you bought the stone from me again?"

And so Ashleaf left the dwarf market, and he took the stone with him, the stone he came there to find. And that was how Ashleaf came to get the stone Winedeep. And for a long time after that, that stone was called Ashleaf's Pride.

The Power of Flight

One day, a man came to the seagull who sits by the seashore. And the man said to the bird: "Tell me, who is that old man I have seen with a sack on his back?"

And the bird said: "It is difficult for me to know which old man you mean. There are many creatures that wander in the world gathering things in sacks. Some might call some of them old. But age is a strange thing. An old man may still appear young to one who is even older. There is some essence of youth that shines through the veils of wrinkles and shrouds of grey. Unsteady steps and faltering voice may not even be noticed by one who is even older. But when youth sees an old man, often he sees only age and nothing else. So I cannot guess which man you mean, or how old he might be.

"Some men catch birds and collect them in the sacks they carry on their backs, thinking that if they have enough birds, they too will be able to fly. Those men do not realise that the power of flight comes not from feathers but from an instinct. It is something those men will never learn."

Great Thoughts

What does it mean to be a god in a land with no men, in a land with no kings and no high priests?

If a god is sustained by the stories that are told about him, who will tell the stories? If no-one is watching as he walks along the lakeshore, thinking great thoughts (or doing any number of great deeds or story-worthy acts), where will the stories come from? Who will tell the stories? Or who is watching and waiting? Or who decides what to tell, or what will be told? These are great thoughts.

If there were eyes watching as Mindrace walked at dusk, grey cloak, grey hood, slowly crossing grey rocks, along the deep grey lake under the red-grey sunset sky, they were not men's eyes. If there were watchers in the shadows, trolls or giants or dwarfs, sitting under the stones, it was not easy for Mindrace to see them. If something moved in the half distance, darting, red-grey, he didn't see whether it was a squirrel or a fox. And if the flicker in the twilight was caused by a flying dragon passing for a moment in front of the setting sun, he didn't see it clearly, and then it was gone, vanished into the pink haze, the vague faraway clouds.

But not everything was quiet. Wavelets slapped water against the stones, wind shushed the papery leaves of the birch trees. And there was the chatter of small birds, who seemed to be following Mindrace everywhere he walked, flying overhead, flitting from tree to tree. They watched, and they chattered between themselves in song.

* * *

Why does the wanderer wander? Does he believe that familiarity with the places he passes will somehow bring them closer to him, that they will somehow belong to him? He circles the whole land. Will he then have claimed everywhere or everything for himself?

It is a slow walk. The landscape changes. He sees whatever there is to see. There are the high fells, each one a different shape. There are bells and towers and steeples, ridge rooves and gables, pikes and pyramids. Some are rounded, grassy tops, some have been bitten to the bare rock. Some shine in the sunlight, silver and gold, others are shrouded by the weather, hooded and hidden by clouds.

He passes lakes too, all of them different. One is long and winding, one is broad. One is round, with many islands. Two small lakes are a pair, twins, linked by a short marshy stream. One is deep and silent, the fellside falls steeply to the water's edge.

He circles the landscape. But there is more to it than this: on his long walk, Mindrace has the time to think.

* * *

Some say that it is the emptiness of men's minds that calls gods into existence. But when the gods themselves wander alone in an empty world, would they not instead call men into existence? For what does it mean to be a god when there is no-one to see it? Mindrace walked along the lakeshore with his thoughts. And men will come here, with their kings and their priests. And they will come soon.

Now is the time to get ready for their coming. Now is the time to decide – when they do come – what stories they will have to tell. They will come soon.

The Myth of Matchless

I know of a dwarf, he sits under the mountain. Many people have heard about this dwarf and what he made. He was a skilled maker, one of the best. Some even say that he worked with Smith in Micklewood. That dwarf is called Matchless. But now all is quiet under the mountain, all is dark.

Long ago, that mountain was called Anvil because of its shape: its flat top and its steep sides. But people also knew that there was a famous smith working there. And when clouds gathered around the top of the mountain, people would say that the smith's fires were burning. But now the mountain is quiet, and it is usually called by another name.

That mountain is now called Goldenchair. Some people say the summit of that mountain resembles a chair. But everyone knows the dragon Goldeneye lives there now, and everyone knows he sits on his hoard of gold under the mountain. And now when the clouds gather around the top of that mountain people say that it is the dragon's fiery breath coming from his underground lair.

There are three great mountains. The first is Skybarrow, which is the highest mountain. That is the place where Farseer sits. The second is Snowbell, which is the name of a flower. In the winter, that mountain is covered in snow. But when the snow melts and spring comes, these white flowers appear on its lower slopes. The third is Trollfell. And the mountain called Anvil is close to Trollfell in the North.

* * *

The dwarf says: I listened to my masters long ago. I heard the words they spoke to me. When I was learning, I listened to them. They taught me everything I know. They taught others before me, and others after me. I know all this. It was only natural that I should believe what they had to say.

Long ago I asked them: You have taught me well, and I have learned many things. Now tell me this: what should I do with all I have learned? Or how can I use these skills when I leave this place? This is the most important lesson. There are many things I could make. I could make a sword of steel, with an edge so sharp and hard that it could easily cut through the blades of lesser swords. The blade would be decorated with patterns of dragon smoke. I see it shining in my mind. Or I could make a gold ring embossed with secret letters. It would bring great power to the one who wore it. Or I could make the most beautiful necklace set with precious stones. It would make the one who wore that necklace very beautiful, and that would bring great power. I can see it in my mind. There are many things I could make. But what should I do?

They told me this: You can do anything you want. You have a special talent, so use it well. The care you take in your work is matchless. The things you make are far beyond what we imagined. There is little point in wasting your time doing things that have been done many times before. Few people will be impressed by seeing the same things made over again. True greatness comes from being the first. There are many makers of swords, rings, jewellery. Unlearn the idea that you should make such things. Do not feel restricted by what you have seen.

You should do something that has not been tried before. Only original creations are rewarded. Whatever you make must stand out from all that came before. It must make people stop and take notice. Be special. Be unique. Everyone remembers the name Smith, because Smith in Micklewood has made the most wonderful treasures, matchless and unique. He does it time and again. But how many dwarfs are there who have made swords and rings? No-one knows their names. These dwarfs are easily forgotten. You could make anything you want. For you there will be no limits. Do not waste your chance to become one of the true greats!

* * *

Tell me then, if you know so much: what was it that the dwarf Matchless made, or what did he bring out from under the mountain?

The dwarf sat for a long time under the mountain. For a long time he thought about everything he knew in the world. Many ideas were abandoned, half-started. "This is too similar to what was made before," he said. "Many dwarfs make swords, necklaces, rings. It hardly matters how well I work if what I make is so common."

So this is what Matchless made. He abandoned all thoughts of metalwork, and instead he began to work on the art of stones. He started to work on creating precious and noble stones, hard crystals, from dust and grit. After some time, he found he was able to tune and temper the colours of the crystals he pulled from the furnace. He polished the clear stones, and he cut the faces, each one a special treasure. And inside, the layers of colour shifted as the stone turned in the light, reflecting different angles and different depths.

This was how Matchless made his Luck. It was a precious jewel the size of a small ball. Around the outside, it was clear and colourless crystal, but peering into the interior revealed clouds of blue. And at the core of it was deep darkness. No-one had seen anything like this before. And it was carved with secret letters that few could read. The Luck was not like fragile glass, but heavy and hard.

* * *

And he brought it out from under the mountain into the sunshine. He walked into the wide valley that lies south of Anvil and north of Fairfell, and he held that stone between his finger and thumb, and he lifted it up into the air. The sun shone into the heart of the stone and it seemed to glow and shine in a way that it had not done when it was underground. And anyone who looked deep into the stone would have marvelled at what they had seen there.

And the dwarf said: "This is what I have made. I call it my Luck. All my skills have gone into this stone, but I have also put into it all my great thoughts, gathered over many years while I sat under the mountain. I have made this for the first time. It is truly unique."

There were other dwarfs there, all of them busy with work. Steel swords and gold rings they made, and fine jewellery. They were happy to show Matchless the things they had made. But no-one was particularly interested in the stone. None of them really knew who he was.

"I have been mainly making swords," one of the dwarfs said. "This is my newest. It is sharp enough that if I hold it still it will cut through leaves blown onto its blade by the wind. I call it Leafwand. I have made other swords: Windwand, Brightstaff, Fellstaff, these are just some of them."

This was the story of the Luck of Matchless. He went back under the mountain, and he took that stone with him. He stayed under the mountain for a long time after that.

Twilight

The time drew on to evening, and day turned to dusk. There came a knock at the door, and when the girl answered, she saw a man standing there wearing travellers' clothes.

"Can you give me food or shelter for the night?" the man asked. And she let him in. That man's name was Scriptor.

The house stood by the shore of a lake that lay in the bottom of a valley in the high fells. A farmer was living in that house with his daughter, and in those days it was not thought of as anywhere special.

"My name is Buttertub," said the farmer. "You must be hungry. Sit down, and my daughter will bring you something to eat."

So Scriptor sat down at the table. The room was rustic and homely. The benches and the table were sturdily built of solid oak, and the plaster walls were painted with flowers and other pictures.

Scriptor said: "Let me tell you why I have come here walking. I am going to write the story of everything. And anyone who reads what I have written will understand everything there is in the world, and all that has happened."

But the farmer and his daughter didn't understand a word Scriptor said because they didn't know what reading was, or writing.

Scriptor said: "Many stories I know. Men have told me many things. Much I have seen as well with my own eyes. And all of it I will write down."

There was a small outbuilding on that farm. And Scriptor went into that small building, and he closed the door behind him.

He had crushed oak galls for ink, and cut birds' feathers for pens. Parchment he had with him also. And Scriptor sat down and he started to write. Once he had started, he hardly stopped.

Outside Scriptor's cell, things were growing darker and greyer. Even when all was darkness outside, Scriptor continued to write.

He worked by candlelight. Many stories he wrote down. Many things he wrote down just as he had heard them. Some things he misremembered. Some things he changed and fixed to improve the story, or to change it back to how it might once have been when the first great storytellers had carefully crafted it. Some of the names in the stories he understood, and those names he wrote down. Some of the names sounded like something he thought he understood, so he wrote down what he thought the names should be. Some of the names were changed so that they would fit better into the stories. Some of the names sounded very vulgar, so he changed those as well.

He worked long into the night, and it was many years' work that needed to be done. So it was a long night that passed before he had finished.

When the new day dawned at last, he left his writing on the table, and he went outside. It was a very different world out there.

It is not fair to say that all trace of the Elders was gone, because they had left things behind. The well-built walls of Highgarth could still be seen, but no-one really knew why they were there or what they were for. The stones the sea-giant had cut to build those walls had started to loosen from one another by the growth of moss and creepers, and they were loosened further by men who prised the stones away and carried them off to build their own houses. The forest at Oakwood was filled only with oaks. It may have been possible to see which of those towering trunks had once held up the roof of Heave's great hall. But only those who searched carefully could see it. High on the fells, enormous boulders sat in the places where once there were giants. The wonder of the smithy in Micklewood had never been easy to find. The waterfall at Forest Force still rang with the sounds of ringing hammers and half-heard calling voices, though the woods seemed empty.

And if there was a place on a high fell where a bird had sat, no-one climbed that fell now. Or if they climbed, it was not to speak to any bird, though there were still places on the fells where big birds could be seen, perching and watching. And if there had been a seagull that flew across the land, no-one searched out that seagull now, to hear its stories. Though there were still many seagulls, flying and wheeling and mewing.

The people who were left in that landscape struggled to remember the way things were before. They tried to tell the old stories as they had always done, but they started to doubt their memories. Something had disappeared.

But the sun shone, the sky was blue, there were flowers everywhere, and the air was filled with the chatter of birdsong.

* * *

Scriptor stayed in that place for some time. And late one night there came a knock at the door. The sun had set long ago in the west, and rosy dawn had not yet begun to approach the eastern edge of the sky. Yet Scriptor was still wide awake. He sat with his manuscript in the middle of the night, and stared at it by candlelight. Scriptor had finished writing. The thing was done. Now he only sat, deep in thought, staring at what he had written. The knock at the door brought him suddenly out of his deep reflection and back into the tiny room.

When Scriptor answered the door, he saw another man who was dressed in just the same way as he was.

"Who comes knocking at this hour of the night?" Scriptor said.

"Have you finished, Scriptor?" said the man.

"Yes, it is finished," said Scriptor. "But how do you know who I am?"

"I would not have come here if I didn't know it," said the man. "I came here to speak to you. You have done well, and soon everyone will know your name and your work. And that is why it is important that everything is just as it should be."

The stacks of parchment were on Scriptor's writing table, all covered in a neat handwriting.

"I would like to read it," said the man. "And I should begin at the beginning."

"Of course." Scriptor handed him the first leaf of parchment. "This is the first part," he said, "about the beginning of everything."

The other man began to read, but he stopped at once.

"This word you've used is no good," he said. "Have you considered that? I am talking about the word that is foremost and first. It could be interpreted in many ways, and I don't suppose any of them are the way you intended. The meaning of that word must not be lost. It must be clear, now, and for as long as this work will endure."

"Perhaps if you read on, it will become clear what I meant when I wrote the first word," said Scriptor.

"I don't think so," said the man. "I am struggling to get past this first word. And I imagine anyone else who tried to read this text would feel the same. This odd and out-of-place word would surely make most people uneasy. No-one will connect with this text. It would be better to use another word here."

"What do you have in mind?" said Scriptor.

"How many words would better convey your meaning! I am surprised you cannot think of any yourself. This hardly fills me with confidence about the rest of the text. I have only read one word of it, that word was wrong, and you seem incapable of correcting it. How many words are there in this work? Many thousands I would imagine. I hope we won't have to go through this process for each one. Perhaps the rest of the words are better chosen than the first, though I hardly dare hope. Now think on this word, and be sure that you have chosen the right one. I will leave you to contemplate your choice."

And then the man disappeared. Scriptor spent many years thinking about the first word of his manuscript, what the word was, and how it would be best to change it.

The other man never returned.